ANTARCTICA
A KAIJU THRILLER
ERIC S BROWN

SEVERED PRESS
HOBART TASMANIA

ANTARCTICA: A KAIJU THRILLER

WWW.SEVEREDPRESS.COM

ISBN: 978-1-925711-06-6

ANTARCTICA: A KAIJU THRILLER

When three guys dressed like the Men in Black come knocking on your office door, it's never a good sign. Only these three guys weren't Men in Black. They were worse, far worse. They had no cool gadgets, didn't police aliens, and usually tended to wreck his life whenever they showed up demanding his help. Sam sighed as they entered, setting aside the papers he had been grading.

"Agent Markson," Sam said, frowning. "What brings you by this time? Did you find some vampires on a cruise ship? Is there a Yeti loose in Louisville? Oh wait…" Sam said, getting up from his chair, gathering up his work, "I know! You've found a dragon sleeping under the streets of London. Am I right?"

"Dr. Jessi," Agent Markson replied, nodding at him. "I understand your skepticism but…"

Sam shook his head violently. "No way are you guys just whisking me out of here again. I've gotten fired from two universities thanks to you already. Do you know how hard it was to get a job again after that last time?"

"I'm sorry that story got leaked to the press, Doctor." Agent Markson looked like he was doing his best not to smirk. "Things like that happen from time to time."

Sam finished cramming his papers into his briefcase and snapped it shut. "Whatever it is, Agent Markson, you can forget it. I'm not interested. I've had enough."

The two men accompanying Agent Markson had spread out to either side of Sam's office door, and he knew they weren't going to let him through it. He could see the bulges of the concealed pistols they were packing beneath their jackets. Sam thought about making a go of it anyway.

"Look, Sam… Can I call you Sam? We've known each other a while now. Like it or not, you're still the leading expert on Kaiju in the States, likely the entire world. We need you," Agent Markson said point blank.

Sam stuck a finger at Agent Markson like a dagger. "I'm a private citizen, Markson. I have rights."

Agent Markson shrugged. "That's cute, Sam. Have you been practicing that?"

Walking past where he stood, Agent Markson plopped himself into the chair Sam had abandoned. "We both know you're coming with us one way or another, Sam. You might as well listen to what I have to say before you opt for it to be the hard way."

"You can't—" Sam started, but Agent Markson cut him off.

"Yes, I can, Sam, and we both know it. If you're done with the theatrics now, I'd like to get down to business." Agent Markson smiled, showing Sam his too white, near perfect teeth.

Sam glanced at the office door again.

"Go ahead and try it, Doctor," one of the two agents said.

"What do you want, Markson?" Sam asked, slamming his briefcase onto the top of his desk.

"We've found a kaiju, Dr. Jessi," Agent Markson said calmly.

"Oh, have you now?" Sam mocked him. "And where did you find a real, live kaiju?"

"I didn't say anything about the kaiju being alive, Dr. Jessi," Agent Markson said with a chuckle.

Against his better judgment, Sam eased himself into the seat in front of his own desk across from Agent Markson. "Okay," he said reluctantly, "I'll bite. You've found a dead kaiju? Seriously?"

"I am very serious, Doctor." Agent Markson leaned forward. "It's the real thing."

"Go on," Sam urged him.

"A research team is in the process of, shall we say, unearthing the kaiju as we speak. We want you there to help oversee the operation and find out all we can about the creature," Agent Markson told him.

Sam's mind was reeling. This time, Agent Markson actually sounded on the up and up. He wasn't asking for Sam's help finding the kaiju and that alone spoke volumes. Every other time Agent Markson had come for him, it was to enlist his help in finding a kaiju or capturing one. To Markson, kaiju was a catch all term for anything that was supernatural or outside of the known parameters of what the real world was supposed to be.

"So you already have the kaiju?" Sam asked, still stunned.

"We do, Dr. Jessi," Agent Markson said, nodding. "And that's why we need you. We need to know what exactly it is. We need to know where it came from. And most of all, we need to know if there are more of them."

The thought of getting to study an honest-to-goodness kaiju corpse was just too good of a chance to pass on if that's really what Markson was offering. Sam had spent his whole life chasing after kaiju. They were everything to him.

Not believing he was actually agreeing to accompany Agent Markson again, Sam said, "I'll need some time to get my affairs in order with the school. I can't afford to lose another job."

"We've already taken care of that," Agent Markson assured him. "Time is of the essence, Doctor. We need to be in route to the kaiju corpse as quickly as we can. I'll tell you more once we're airborne."

"Fine," Sam agreed. "But I get the window seat in the copter this time."

Agent Markson laughed. "Consider it yours."

"And I get to pick the flight music this time too," Sam demanded. "No more of that metal crap you guys like to blast so much."

Agent Markson flinched and then shook his head. "If that's what it takes to keep from having to have my men break some of your bones to get you moving, you've got a deal."

Sam leapt up from his seat. "Well, then, Agent Markson, what in the devil are we waiting on? Take me to your kaiju!"

****

Colonel Pitt stood on the railing of the small balcony-like area of the hastily constructed base that rested in the earth next to the Cavern. The base served primarily as living quarters and storage for the crew that he and his men had accompanied to Antarctica. Work on the base had started almost a year ago and it was nearing completion. The amount of money and resources both the government and military had poured into it was staggering. Of course, the real work was being done in the Cavern itself. That was where the scientists harvested their samples and continued their efforts to ever so carefully thaw out the body of the giant monster that rested within it. As vast as the Cavern was, in truth, it only contained about forty percent of the monster's body. The rest of the thing's corpse remained inaccessible for the time being, buried in the ice, beyond the reach of the scientists. The Cavern grew each day but at such a slow rate it was impossible to tell with the naked eye to Colonel Pitt. He was the military liaison attached to the project and had no training in the type of archeological work that was being conducted in extracting the monster's gigantic body from the ice. He supposed he had been assigned the job because he did hold a degree in General Science. His interest in science was nothing more than a hobby, something he read about for fun and pleasure, and he hadn't done anything useful with his degree in his entire life. He had used the military to pay for his degree but upon completing it had decided to re-enter active service. Over the last decade, Pitt had fought and worked his way up the ranks to becoming the full-fledged colonel he currently was. If the higher ups really believed that his degree gave him a better understanding of the work taking place in the Cavern, he wanted some of what they had to be smoking. The work being done in the Cavern was so far over his head that to think his little degree would allow him to fully understand it was laughable.

The base adjoining the Cavern was simply referred to as Alpha Station by the men who were stationed within its walls. The entire base and the Cavern itself were subterranean, heated and powered by huge turbine generators that ran off a sort of mini-nuclear reactor paid for by one of the private corporations who were also helping to bankroll the project. Colonel Pitt doubted very much that the reactor was even legal, but the experts who watched over it assured him that it was safe. Regardless, he was thankful for the closed environment and the heat. Above ground, the temperature this time of year floated around the minus fifty degrees mark. At least down here in Alpha Station, he didn't have to deal with the cold or the sudden ice storms that seemed to roll in from out of nowhere.

There were two dozen Special Forces operatives and two pilots under his command in total. It was a small force but a hardcore one. His men were the best of the best. Colonel Pitt had handpicked each and every one of them. They weren't lacking in weapons or supplies either, which was something he had sometimes dealt with in the Sandbox. In addition to the arsenal tucked away in Alpha Station, Colonel Pitt had two Mi-8AMTSh-VA arctic helicopters at his disposal, as well as three modified-for-the-cold APCs. If anything went wrong, he felt confident that he had the firepower at hand to deal with it.

In addition to his own men, Alpha Station was home to twenty science personnel and another two dozen grunt workers and equipment operators/techs. Very few of them complained much about the Spartan living conditions of Alpha Station. The science folks were too busy with their "find" to care about much else, and the workers were getting paid such enormous sums for their time, labor, and above all, discretion, that they would be set for years when their work here was finished.

Dr. Ashley Hall was the head of the science team, and Chief "Rigger" Waters was in charge of the works and techs. Colonel Pitt respected both of them. "Rigger" was the sort of chief engineer that every CO prayed they have under their command. He was efficient, friendly, and willing to compromise when the need to do so arose, as long as that compromise didn't put himself and his workers at risk. Rigger was in his early forties and had worked all over the globe. He was a big man, standing over six feet tall and all muscle from head to toe. His red hair only added to his friendly appearance. Rigger would never be handsome but the man had cute down to an art form. His last job had been helping to build a large undersea research station for a private corporation that was intent on exploring the ocean trenches of the Pacific Rim. Rigger was as close to perfect as anyone could ask for to head up the work being done in the Cavern. Dr. Hall, on the other hand, was very set in her ways and used to being in charge. The fact that she shared command here with himself and Rigger bothered her greatly at times. Colonel Pitt had no doubt she was an expert in xenobiology. She wouldn't be allowed to be in charge over the science team if she wasn't. The woman held a staggering number of degrees for her young years. According to her file, Dr. Hall was thirty-four but she looked like she was in her mid-twenties. She might be a nerd, but Dr. Hall had the figure of a super model. She was a thin, well-toned, five-foot-four bundle of energy that never seemed to become exhausted. Colonel Pitt had once joked that if you looked up overachiever in the dictionary, you'd find her picture next to the word's definition. He and Dr. Hall didn't see eye to eye on a lot of things regarding the handling of the specimen housed, still mostly frozen and buried in the Cavern, but so far their disagreements were minor ones, and he hoped that they stayed that way.

It was all insane when you thought it about, at least the way Colonel Pitt saw things. The thing in the Cavern wasn't an active threat. It was long dead and frozen. Dr. Hall's best estimate put its death occurring sometime around the beginning of the ice age. If there were creatures like it still out there, they were doing a heck of a job keeping themselves hidden from the world, especially considering their size. Odds were, if things like the monster in the Cavern had existed, they were long gone. Colonel Pitt wasn't entirely convinced that the thing was even from Earth. How it looked alone was a strong argument for it being alien. Nonetheless, the higher ups wanted to know as much about the creature as they could. If they were still out there somewhere or returned one day, someone was surely going to have to take them on. The eerie feeling he got just looking at the monster told him that it and any others like it were hostile and would certainly be looking for a fight.

Dr. Hall assured him that the monster's corpse and the ice it was frozen in were clear of any nasty bugs or dormant viruses that might be a threat to those working in the cavern. Colonel Pitt believed that Dr. Hall knew her business, but he wasn't taking any chances. Those that worked directly with the monster's tissues or had direct contact with the ice it was frozen in were made to suit up in hazmat gear and go through decontamination when their shifts were done. There was simply no reason not to cover all the bases from the get go. He had watched enough B horror movies to know how fast things could go wrong and get out of control if there was some sort of strange virus in the beast's blood. Thankfully, despite her belief that the beast and the ice were clean, Dr. Hall was professional enough to know that he was right and enforcing such safety protocols was a good idea. Chief Rigger and his men actually complained about the suits a great deal more than the science team. They weren't all used to working in such suits. They claimed they were uncomfortable and slowed down their work. Rigger made sure all his people complied with the protocols though.

Word was that the higher ups had decided to bring in an expert who supposedly knew about the monster to assist Dr. Hall. Colonel Pitt could tell she was ticked off about it. She didn't feel she needed any help. Colonel Pitt had to admit that Dr. Hall had indeed made some good progress in learning about the monster given that she was starting from a level-zero knowledge base. It just wasn't fast enough progress he figured for those footing the bills. This new guy that was being flown in wasn't on her level in terms of "real science" Dr. Hall had told him. Colonel Pitt had barely been able to keep his laughter to himself when she told him the new guy was a cryptozoologist with a specialty in kaiju. The sad part was that it wasn't really funny. When the military sunk to employing folks like that, it was just depressing. The new guy was slated to arrive later tonight via copter from the *USS Penton*.

Colonel Pitt stared at one of the monster's large, glazed over, half frozen, yellow eyes, which was much larger than he was, trying again to make sense of it all. No matter how hard he tried, he just couldn't really come to terms with that fact that monster in the Cavern was real. When it was alive, the thing had stood close to six hundred feet high. Its skin was dense enough to shrug off anything short of tank-level AP rounds and even those were likely only to make it mad until you hit with enough to make it bleed out. A chill ran along his spine, and he shuddered at the thought of ever really having to fight one of the monsters. He didn't doubt that something like it could be killed, but the amount of firepower and time it would take to take it down... Only God knew how many lives would be lost before the thing finally bled out and died. The other option was, of course, to nuke something like it, but that option came with a whole other set of nightmares attached to it.

Tearing his eyes away from the monster, Colonel Pitt noticed he was clutching the railing of the balcony in a white-knuckled grip. He let go of it, interlocking his hands to pop his finger joints. It felt good to do so and blunted the edge of the nervousness he was feeling. Thanking God that they found the thing dead instead of alive, he turned and left the balcony, heading back inside the base. There was a bottle of vodka waiting for him in the drawer of his desk, and if there was ever a reason to knock a glass back, it was staring into the eye of a monster straight out of the worst sort of Japanese legend.

Colonel Pitt hoped the new guy could find whatever information the higher ups were looking for fast because he was so done with this place and all the insanity that came with it. As much as he hated playing babysitter to Dr. Hall and Chief Rigger's crews, he hated being near that thing in the Cavern more. As long as he lived, he was never going to be able to forget that monster, no matter how much he tried. He prayed that when the science geeks and the higher ups had whatever they needed from its body that they were going to let him blow the freaking thing to bits because he figured it was going to take that in order from him to sleep properly again someday, if he ever did.

****

Dr. "Sam" Jessi sat staring out the window of the small helicopter. Agent Markson sat in its rear with him. Other than the two pilots in the bird's front, they were alone. They both wore headsets so that they could talk during the ride, but Agent Markson had kept quiet, and Sam was fascinated by the endless sea of white that stretched on into the horizon in every direction. Agent Markson had dragged him to some strange places but Antarctica… It was something else. Of all the places in the world, Sam would have never have considered Antarctica a possibility when it came to discovering a kaiju. The more he thought about it, the more it seemed like a bad H.P. Lovecraft story. According to Agent Markson, a research team had found the body of a kaiju buried in the ice a little over a year ago. A great deal of effort and money had been spent on building a makeshift base around the kaiju's corpse, as it was simply too massive to extract from the ice as a whole. There were already other scientists at the site studying the creature, and it made Sam wonder why Agent Markson had waited so long to contact him.

"Quite a sight out there, isn't it?" Agent Markson asked, gesturing at the snow and ice.

"Breathtaking," Sam agreed.

"This is the real deal, Sam," Agent Markson assured him. "I imagine it's the chance of a lifetime for someone like you."

"I've heard that from you before, Markson," Sam replied, frowning.

"Did I tell you who is in charge of the science team already on site?" Agent Markson grinned, and Sam knew whatever he was about to say wasn't going to be good news.

"No. Who?" Sam asked.

"I think you know her," Agent Markson said, stretching out his big reveal. "It's Dr. Hall."

"Ashley Hall?" Sam's eyes bugged and his mouth fell open.

"That's her," Agent Markson said with a smirk. "The one and only."

"Fantastic." Sam's sarcasm dripped from how he said the word. He knew Ashley well. She was a large part of the reason that so much of the scientific community didn't take his work seriously. The two of them had never gotten along. "Have you told her you're bringing me in on this?"

Agent Markson nodded. "Trust me, she was overjoyed to hear the news."

"I bet so," Sam grunted in response.

The base came into view outside the helicopter's window as the pilot circled in for a landing. Sam frowned as he looked it over. There were only three buildings. One looked to be some kind of power plant and was the largest of the three. The other resembled small Arctic habits like he had seen on TV and in movies. The smallest one reminded Sam of an outhouse in its size and shape.

Agent Markson must have noticed his expression because he said, "The real base is underground. I thought I told you that. You won't believe what we've been able to do here when you see it."

Sam nodded, not really believing Markson as the helicopter touched down. There were two men waiting on them as Sam tugged his parka tighter about his body and exited the helicopter with Agent Markson following after him.

One of the men was clearly a military man. His posture and how he moved assured Sam that the man was not the type of person you wanted to tick off. The other man had a more ragged look about him. He was huge. The Arctic gear he wore only added to his already imposing stature. He truly would have been intimidating, but there was a friendly aura about him, enhanced by his boyish looks, that put Sam at ease as he stepped forward.

"You must be Dr. Jessi!" he big man yelled over the noise of the helicopter's settling blades. "I'm Chief Rigger and this is Colonel Pitt! He's in charge here."

"Agent Markson," Colonel Pitt said, nodding in greeting. "It's good to have you back."

"I guess we'd better all stop standing around out here like idiots in the rain and get inside before we freeze," Chief Rigger said with a laugh.

Chief Rigger led the group of four towards the smallest of the three topside buildings. Its door slid open as they approached it. Its interior was well heated and the sharp change in temperature was shocking to Sam. It felt good though. Sam promised himself that was never going outside again until it was time to head back to the States when the project's work was completed. Despite his parka, his teeth were chattering, and he was shivering even though he was beginning to warm up. His nose felt like a cube of ice that was glued to his face.

"The cold out there takes some getting used to," Chief Rigger told him. "You don't want to be caught out in it."

Sam looked around at the interior of the building. It was just as small as it looked to be from the outside. The only thing in it was a set of elevator style doors at its far side. There was a security lock keypad next to the doors, and Chief Rigger hurriedly typed a six-digit sequence of numbers on it. When he was done, the doors opened into what appeared to be a lift.

"Going down?" Chief Rigger said, smiling at Sam as he ushered him into the lift.

The lift lurched and started moving as soon as they were all inside it. The trip down was a short one. The doors opened into a metal-walled corridor with lights strung across its ceiling. Sam followed the others along it for a short ways before they took a turn to the right and stepped out onto a balcony overlooking the heart of the base. The balcony overlooked a large, wide-open work area, and within it was the most wonderful, terrifying thing Sam had ever seen in his life. His mouth fell open as he stared at the kaiju, partially uncovered from the ice that surrounded the rest of its body.

"We call this part of the base the Cavern," Colonel Pitt said, but Sam wasn't really listening to him.

"She's beautiful," Sam muttered unable to take his gaze away from the kaiju.

"I guess that's one way to put it," Chief Rigger said, chuckling.

"Dr. Hall is sorry she was unable to welcome you to the base, but she's busy as we speak with her work," Colonel Pitt told him.

Yeah, I bet she is, Sam thought. *And I don't blame her.*

"When can I get down there?" Sam asked, not even bothering to try to hide the excitement and eagerness he was feeling.

Agent Markson leaned over and whispered, "Told ya so. This one is going to make your career."

"I think it is best that you have some knowledge of what Dr. Hall has learned from the kaiju's corpse so far before you join her in her work, Dr. Jessi. No one wants any setbacks simply because you are new here and don't know the procedures we use." Colonel

Pitt eyed him. "I am told your expertise is a bit more esoteric than Dr. Hall's."

"I would say that's relative, Colonel," Sam replied, shrugging. "She's more hard science in a practical sense, yes, but she doesn't know kaiju like I do. I've studied their legends and history my entire life."

"I see," Colonel Pitt commented, utterly unimpressed.

"Look, I know you want to stay here and keep ogling that thing, Sam," Agent Markson cut in, "but there'll be plenty of time for that sort of thing later on. Right now, let's get you to your quarters."

Sam didn't want to leave the balcony, but he knew Agent Markson was right. The sooner he got situated and settled in, the sooner he could get his hands on the kaiju corpse. He trembled with an almost orgasmic joy at the thought.

"Sure," Sam agreed, taking one last, long look at the monstrous thing embedded in the ice of the Cavern before letting Agent Markson lead him away from the balcony.

****

As Sam and Agent Markson strolled through the corridors of the base, they occasionally passed some workers scurrying by. The base was both larger and more populated than Sam had expected. It truly was an impressive structure to have been built in such a short time. It had rough edges to it though, which made it clear there was still a lot of work to be done. Sam imagined that work on the base was by far secondary to the further extraction and study of the kaiju corpse, however. This section of the base appeared to be mostly quarters. Agent Markson explained that the base built around the Cavern actually had three levels to it and was called Alpha Station. The top level was mostly quarters as Sam suspected, given his own was on it, but it was also home to the administrative section containing a communications room, two meeting rooms, and the base's mess hall and kitchen. The second level contained several labs and was where the armory for Colonel Pitt and his men were housed. The third level down was a mix of equipment storage and a series of rooms where the larger pieces from the kaiju corpse were kept and studied.

Sam found his quarters to be just as Spartan as he thought they would be when he and Agent Markson arrived at them. They consisted of a small room with an adjoining bathroom. Inside the room, there was only a bed, a work desk, with a chair scooted beneath the desk, and a small trunk where his personal belongings could be stored. Sam was glad he hadn't brought much with him. All he had brought were his laptop, a few carefully selected volumes on kaiju lore, and a couple of changes of clothing. Most folks that he had seen in Alpha Station so far wore uniforms denoting which of the base's three groups of personnel they belonged to. Colonel Pitt's men wore green, military fatigues, while Chief Rigger's workers wore construction uniforms, and Dr. Hall's staff was dressed in lab coats.

There were some though who wore normal civilian clothing such as casual T-shirts and jeans, but they were in the minority. It could have been they were simply off-duty at the time he had seen them, but he doubted that explained them all. Science geeks and construction workers loved their T-shirts, and even in them, it was easy to tell who belonged to which group. A science geek likely wouldn't be caught dead in a John Deere tractor shirt nor would a construction geek normally being wearing an Albert Einstein shirt with a quote about relativity on it and complex equations on the back. Sam knew he was stereotyping, but even so, he would wager a guess based on one of the shirts that he would be correct two out of three times down here.

"Home sweet home," Sam said with a laugh as he walked into his quarters and placed his single bag at the foot of its bed.

"I think you'll fit right in here, Sam," Agent Markson said, flashing his too white teeth in a wide smile. "No password for the Wi-Fi but no external lines of communication either without approval from myself or Colonel Pitt. Anything else you need to know about Alpha Station, that's not classified, you can find in the info packet I had the colonel email you."

"Thanks," Sam replied.

Sam stopped the government agent as he turned to leave. "No, Markson, I mean it. Really, thanks for this one."

Agent Markson flashed him another smile and then was gone, disappearing into the corridor beyond the room. Sam closed the door after him. As he did so, he realized the door was pure steel, as it took some effort to move. Markson hadn't had any trouble opening it as they entered, but for Sam, it was a challenge. Sam supposed he should find it comforting that Markson was in such good shape, as he would be serving as Alpha Station's security government liaison and making sure that Pitt's men didn't abuse their power as the base's protectors. Lying to himself that he would start working out more, Sam knelt next to the room's bed and dug his laptop out of his bag.

Sam was tired but knew he was far too excited to sleep. He had just seen a real, if dead, kaiju with his own eyes. Taking a seat at the desk, he powered up his laptop and quickly read through the info packet the colonel had emailed him before beginning his work. There were tons of kaiju descriptions out there in stories passed down from one generation to the next and legends all across history of giant monsters that had once walked the Earth. Sam started poring through them to see if he could find any whose description matched the appearance of the kaiju corpse he had just seen. It was as good a starting point as any. He managed two solid hours of research without finding anything in the legends and stories that resembled the corpse in the Cavern.

Yawning, Sam closed his laptop and got up from the desk. He was exhausted from the hurried journey and the emotional high of seeing a real kaiju corpse. Plopping onto the edge of the room's bed, he removed his boots and socks. He set the alarm on his phone to wake him up in a couple of hours and sprawled out on top of the bed's sheets. Alpha Station was well heated and sleep came easily to him. He was out almost as soon as his eyes closed.

Sam dreamed of monsters and days gone by. He walked the Earth with primitive cave dwelling tribes who painted pictures of the great kaiju on their walls. Sam stood in the streets of Rome watching a two-hundred-foot-tall kaiju crashing its way through the city as people fled its path of destruction. Then he was in the American Old West. A bounty hunter and his hired guns loaded a Gatling gun outside the mouth of an abandoned mine, preparing for the monster they had tracked there to emerge from its depths. There was a case of dynamite on hand should the Gatling, rifles, and shotguns not be enough to bring the kaiju down. The scene in his mind changed once again as Sam ran for his life across the deck of cruise ship. Tentacles rose over its sides, reaching for the passengers aboard it. As one them found him, snapping him up into the air, Sam awoke with a scream. It echoed off the walls of the small room as he bolted up in the bed. The sheets under him were soaked with sweat. He was in the process of shaking his head to clear it and realizing it was all just a dream as a knock clanged against the room's door.

Jumping up from the bed, Sam ran his hands over his hair trying to straighten it up as much as he could. There was no time for a shower. He grabbed some deodorant from his bag, smeared it over his chest beneath his shirt, and then tossed it back inside.

The knocking at the door grew louder as he rushed over to open it. His eyes bugged with surprise as he found Dr. Ashley Hall standing in the corridor waiting on him.

"Ashley," Sam blurted out.

She looked him up and down then snorted. "I see some things never change, Sam. You always were a mess."

"Look... Uh... I just got here," Sam tried to explain. "I haven't been here more than a few hours."

"It was Agent Markson's idea to bring you in on this, Sam, not mine," Dr. Hall said, emphasizing the last two words. "I've made some pretty remarkable discoveries about this 'kaiju' in the Cavern. It's unlike any other organism on this planet in many respects. I don't want you screwing up what we're accomplishing here. You need to understand right from the start that I, not you, am the head of this science team here. Do I make myself clear?"

Sam found himself smirking. Ashley always was cute when she was upset. It was something about the intense squint around the corners of her eyes. As much as he disliked her, he really liked her too. It was one of the paradoxes of his life, he supposed. He resented her for how she had attacked his work, but he also remembered the days they were friends what seemed like an eternity ago in college. Seeing her in person and having her standing so close to him, it was hard to think about anything but the good times really. Well, at least when she wasn't yelling at him.

"Sam!" she snapped at him as he continued to stare at her like a dummy.

"Oh... Uh... Right." Sam tried to wipe the smirk from his face and focus. "No issues from me, Ashley. I don't think anything that I will be working on would conflict with your own work anyway."

"It's Dr. Hall," she said in a very cold voice.

"Sure," Sam answered. "I didn't mean to be unprofessional."

"Colonel Pitt has a briefing planned at eighteen hundred hours to bring you up to speed on what we've been doing here. Make sure you're there," she told him and then called over her shoulder as she walked away, "and on time, Sam! The colonel isn't the kind of man you want to get on the wrong side of."

Her warning given, she disappeared around a bend in the corridor as Sam leaned out of the doorway of his quarters watching her go. *That went well*, he mocked himself as he stepped back inside and shut the door. In truth, it could have gone far, far worse, and he knew it. He had gotten off easy all things considered.

****

By the time Sam had showered and gotten his clothes changed, he was already on the verge of being late for the briefing the colonel had arranged for him. He tore out of his quarters, sprinting through the corridors of Alpha Station until he suddenly realized he had no idea where he was going. In a panic, he froze not knowing what to do. If he went back to his quarters to bring up the specs for the base on his laptop and tried to find the briefing room that way, he knew he would be even later than he already was. A soldier and one of Chief Rigger's work crew were walking along the corridor up ahead of him. Sam charged them, his expression wild and frantic.

"Whoa," the soldier told him. "Slow down, buddy."

"Do know where the colonel is?" Sam blurted at him.

"He's in conference room A," the soldier answered. "You're new here, aren't you?"

Sam wanted to grab the soldier and shake him until he told him where the room was but knew that would only end up with the man beating the crap out of him most likely. The guy was a trained fighter and he was just a cryptozoological scholar.

"Yeah, I'm new here," Sam answered. "Look, I don't have time to talk. I just need to know where that room is. Please."

"It's around the corner over there, fourth room on the left," the worker told him.

"Thank you," Sam shouted as he ran in the direction the worker had gestured towards.

He heard the soldier and the worker saying something about *crazy newbies* as he left them behind him in his panicked flight. As far as he was concerned, they could think whatever they wanted to about him. He just had to get to that meeting.

Finally, Sam found the briefing room. He checked his watch and saw that it was two minutes past eighteen hundred hours. Despite his best efforts, he was late as usual. Ashley was going to kill him even if the colonel didn't. Taking a deep breath, he tried to calm himself and opened the door, entering the briefing room.

"Glad you could join us, Dr. Jessi," a cold voice growled at him. It belonged to Colonel Pitt, sitting at the table in the center of the room with Agent Markson, Ashley, and Chief Rigger. "Dr. Hall had informed us that you would be running a few minutes late."

Sam shot a look at Ashley. He didn't know whether to feel insulted or thankful.

"Yes, sir. I wanted to make sure I was fully prepared for this meeting," Sam lied.

"Take a seat," Chief Rigger said, gesturing at the empty chair at the end of the table opposite the one Colonel Pitt was sitting in at the table's head.

Sliding into the chair, Sam tried to say something that sounded intelligent. "I've been poring through my files trying to find a match for the kaiju corpse you've discovered."

Sam heard Ashley huff at his claim. The frown on her face was truly an epic one even for her.

"And what purpose will doing that serve, Dr. Jessi?" Colonel Pitt asked.

"Well, sir, for starters, it will tell us where this kaiju came from I hope," Sam explained. "Though kaiju appear to be reptilian and therefore cold-blooded, not all of them truly are. Still, I highly doubt it is native to this region. This kaiju you've found could have come from anywhere and simply had the bad luck of getting frozen here. There are no legends that I know of that contain stories of kaiju in Antarctica."

"I still don't understand how that will help us," the colonel said.

Sam stared at him for a moment, searching for the right words. "If we know which kaiju you've found, it will help us to better understand what it is and give Dr. Hall and her staff a better starting point in their work."

"We started our work months ago, Sam," Ashley reminded him.

Colonel Pitt raised an eyebrow at her use of his first name but kept quiet.

"I know," Sam admitted, "but at this point, you and your team are just taking blind stabs in the dark at finding out what you can about the kaiju. Knowing its origins and what it is will help you refine your work."

"I'm not sure you understand what we're trying to accomplish here, Dr. Jessi," Colonel Pitt told him. "There are really only two things that the people paying for all this care about. One, are there more of these creatures that might be alive and out there hiding somewhere today and two, how do we kill them?"

Sam blinked, stunned about the colonel's blunt declaration.

"Those are very important things to know, I'll admit that," Sam said, "but there is so much more we can learn given the opportunity we have here, Colonel. Aren't you at least somewhat curious as to where the kaiju came from?"

"Only if it helps us determine if there are more of them out there, Doctor," Colonel Pitt answered, leaning forward in his chair to clasp his hands together on the tabletop.

"I don't see how that's honestly even a question that needs to be answered, Colonel." Sam was getting frustrated by military man's single-mindedness. "There are too many stories and legends about kaiju, from all over the globe, to think that the corpse you have found is an isolated aberration of some kind."

"There are countless sightings of Bigfoot too," Agent Markson spoke up. "But as yet, there is no hard evidence that Sasquatch exist."

"This isn't some paranormal investigative TV show, Sam," Ashley launched into him. "This is real life. I don't even understand why Agent Markson insisted on bringing you here. You have nothing to offer that my team and myself aren't capable of doing without you."

"You're wrong, Dr. Hall," Agent Markson argued. "Sam knows more about kaiju lore than anyone else alive. If he can find legends that mention this creature, then right there is the proof that the corpse is likely not an isolated case. And once he's found that, it will give us a good idea of where to look for more of the monsters."

"You're putting a lot of faith in Sam." Sam met Agent Markson's eyes. "I wouldn't if I were you."

"Tell me, Dr. Hall, just how much have you and your team found out about that kaiju in the Cavern's origins? Have you found anything so far that tells you if there are more of them?" Agent Markson demanded.

"Well... No," Dr. Hall admitted, "but look at we have discovered it."

"I have read your reports, Dr. Hall," Agent Markson said, smirking. "You have indeed discovered some things about what makes it tick. I'll give you that. But even in that regard, you haven't been able to conclusively say if it's native to Earth or not. Though some of its genetic and physiological traits appear alien, they could be from the unknown depths of this planet's oceans just as easily as they could be extraterrestrial in nature. Heck, if you really wanted to stretch things, we could even speculate that the kaiju in the Cavern is a bio-engineered weapon of some advanced civilization that predates mankind on this planet and remains as yet unknown to us."

"Be all that as it may," Colonel Pitt interrupted taking control of the room. "What matters is answering the two questions I mentioned. Those are what we're here for. Let's none of us forget it either."

Everyone was silent as Colonel Pitt glanced around the table making sure they all understood he meant what he said.

"Dr. Hall, I want you to continue your work on finding out all you about the kaiju in a biological sense. Dr. Jessi, it's up to you it seems to tell me if the United States, the world even, needs to be gearing up to go to war with monsters like that one in the Cavern someday." Colonel Pitt gestured at Chief Rigger and Agent Markson. "These two will help you in any way they can. Just let them know of your needs as they arise. Now, we have wasted enough time here already. Dr. Hall, you can brief Dr. Jessi yourself on the protocols he needs to follow when working in your labs and the Cavern itself."

"Yes, sir," Ashley answered reluctantly.

Sam had to wonder if she had hoped to get him kicked out of the project during his meeting from the level of disappointment she appeared to have. If she did, she had failed. Clearly, Colonel Pitt was at least willing to give him a chance to prove his usefulness in the study of the kaiju.

"Get back to work, people," Colonel Pitt growled, dismissing them all. "The clock is ticking. A live one of those things could show up at anytime, anywhere, and we need to be ready if that happens."

As everyone filed out of the briefing room, Ashley waited on him.

"Come on then," she said. "Let's get this over with."

Chief Rigger accompanied them. He gave Sam a quick talk about how things operated in the Cavern, what areas were off-limits except to his workers and which were not. He also showed Sam the hazmat-like suits that he and his men wore when they worked near exposed kaiju scales and flesh that wasn't still frozen in the ice. The suits were self-contained with their own power supplies, helmet radios, and air supplies. The only difference between them and other suits of their like that Sam could see was that they were made tougher. According to Chief Rigger, the suits were much more difficult to tear and somewhat akin to light armor. Chief Rigger said the suits were indeed based on a prototype of self-contained armor that the military was working on. There really wasn't a need for the extra level of protection as things turned out, but no one had known that when the project was being put together and he claimed they made his men feel safer when working in the Cavern.

According to the bits of Alpha Station's logs that Agent Markson had sent him, along with the information packet on the base from the colonel in his email, there were several cases of personnel being shipped back stateside because they had been deemed psychologically unfit for the work or experienced outright nervous breakdowns from seeing the kaiju's corpse or having to work so close to it. Sam could believe it too. The kaiju was so monstrous that it likely made the workers scurrying about the Cavern feel like insects compared to it. Sam found the kaiju perversely beautiful. It was the realization of his life's work. Even so, the images of its glazed-over, gigantic yellow eyes haunted him.

When Chief Rigger had finished going over the basics of working in the Cavern and the suits, Sam found himself left alone with Ashley. The chief returned to work, overseeing another section of ice that was being removed from the kaiju as Ashley led Sam on to give him a tour of the base's lab facilities.

The whole experience was a draining as it was exciting. Sam was glad when it was over and thankful that he was going to have a lab to himself. Ashley had made sure to pick the smallest and crudest of the labs for him, but it fit him just fine. It had the gear to do any hands on work he might need to do with samples from the corpse and provided a private space, outside of his own quarters, where he could do his research. Best of all, it was the closest lab to the Cavern itself. All he had to do was step outside its door and take a few steps to the right in order to enter the edge of the Cavern so that he could look on the great beast with his own eyes.

Sam could tell Ashley was glad to be rid of him as they parted for the evening. He wished her a pleasant night and got no response before finding through the corridors of Alpha Station back to his quarters. As soon as he entered them and closed the door, he stretched his arms over his head, helping to relax their tired muscles. With a start, he realized he hadn't had dinner. In fact, he couldn't even remember the last time he had eaten anything. His stomach grumbled at him. Running his fingers through his hair, he knew he had to make a choice. He could head out again to the base's mess hall and hope that there was some food available at this time in the evening to be had there, or he could he could just crash and stuff himself at breakfast in the morning. Sam decided quickly that going in search of food was the thing to do. Not only was he unlikely to sleep well without it, but doing so would give him a chance to perhaps meet more of the people who called Alpha Station home for the time being.

The mess hall was easy to locate. The lights strung up along the ceiling of the base's corridors stayed on 24/7 based on what he read about the base. The corridors were empty. He hadn't realized just how late it had gotten to be. While work continued in the Cavern around the clock with Chief Rigger's men working shifts, the rest of Alpha Station appeared to mostly shutdown during the nighttime hours. Sam counted himself lucky that were lights still on in the base's mess as he entered it. Apparently, it remained open at all times, despite having designated times for the three, real meals of the day. The mess only had two other occupants. One of them was a man much older than Sam with graying hair pulled into a rough ponytail and a beak-like nose. The other was a young woman who appeared to be in her twenties. They were dressed in civilian clothes so it was impossible to tell which of the three groups that made up Alpha Station's residents they belonged to. Both of them looked up and in his direction as he approached them.

"Hi," Sam announced himself. "I'm…"

"You're the new egghead they just flew in," the old man finished for him. "Dr. Jessi, ain't it?"

Sam nodded as the old man rose from his seat to offer him his hand. Clasping it, Sam shook with the old man and then released his hold as they both took seats at the table where the young woman was still sitting.

"You can call me Frank and this is Lieutenant Caroline Edwards," the old man said, smiling as he introduced the young woman. "She's military but don't let that scare you off. She won't bite."

Caroline laughed at the introduction the old man had given her. "Welcome to Alpha Station, Dr. Jessi." She nodded in greeting. "I'm not one of Colonel Pitt's grunts, if that's what you're wondering. I fly the helicopters you saw out there on your way in."

"Actually, I didn't notice them to tell the truth," Sam admitted and wondered how he had overlooked the helicopters she was talking about.

"And you shouldn't have." Caroline grinned. "They're decked out in arctic camo. Besides, I'm sure you were likely a bit overwhelmed at the time. Most people are when they first get here if they've never been to the Arctic before."

"Yeah, I suppose you're right," Sam agreed. His attention had been focused on the buildings of the exterior part of Alpha Station when he arrived and then he rushed inside the main base itself before he froze to death.

"So what do you do here, Frank?" Sam asked.

"I'm part of the chief's team," Frank told him. "I'm one of the folks who keep Alpha Station's power flowing."

Sam noticed that the two of them didn't have any food. Frank had a large mug of coffee clutched in his hands and Caroline was sipping on an energy drink. He looked around the mess.

"If you're looking for dinner, you're a bit late." Caroline grinned at him. "There are some small boxes of cereal and snack stuff over there though."

She pointed at a short cluster of tables that ran along the mess hall's left side.

"Thanks," Sam said. "Excuse me just a moment."

Sam got up and went over to the tables. He wasn't fan of cereal, dry or otherwise. Thankfully, there was an assortment of snack cakes, granola bars, and power bars on the tables too. Grabbing up two snake cakes, he tore the wrapper from one and shoved it into his mouth, scarfing it down as he spotted the two coffee pots nearby. There were mugs placed next to them. Sam filled one up to its brim and carried it to the table where Caroline and Frank were still sitting with his remaining snack cake.

"Breakfast of champions," he joked, as he opened his second snack cake.

"Ain't it though?" Frank agreed.

"You're a cryptozoologist, huh?" Caroline asked.

"Yep," Sam answered, attempting to smile around the snack cake that filled his mouth.

"What is that exactly?" Frank asked him.

"The short answer is that I study monsters," Sam answered.

"Sounds like a fun job," Caroline said.

"It has its ups and downs," Sam admitted.

"So is this an up or a down?" Caroline asked.

"I'm not sure yet," Sam answered her honestly. "I am leaning towards an up though. I've spent my entire life searching for creatures like that one in the Cavern. To finally find one and know that things like it are real, well, it's sort of like a dream come true."

"Or a nightmare come to life," Frank replied with a smirk. "Have you ever seen that famous monster movie about a thing like that one in the Cavern rampaging through the streets of Japan? It didn't go too well for the Japanese."

Sam laughed. "No, I guess it didn't."

"Sometimes it's best to be careful what you wish for, Dr. Jessi," Frank told him. "There are enough monsters in this world already."

"Really, call me Sam," he said, dodging the rest of Frank's comment. "Say, why are you guys up so late anyway?"

"I'm on my way topside to check on things up there." Frank slid his chair back as he got up. "There's a storm rolling in. It was nice to meet you, Sam. I hope you find whatever it is you're looking for here."

"I already have," Sam said, beaming as he thought of the kaiju corpse. He watched Frank as the older man headed out of the mess hall then turned to Caroline, "And what about you?"

"Couldn't sleep," Caroline answered mischievously.

"Well, I don't think that's going to help get the job done," Sam said, gesturing at the energy drink she was sipping on.

"No, probably not," Caroline agreed, "but then who needs sleep?"

Caroline got up. "You take care of yourself, Sam. I'm sure I'll see you around. Alpha Station isn't that big of a place."

"You too." Sam nodded at her and then was left alone with only his coffee for company.

****

Dustin sat in the Cavern's systems control room. He had chugged another cup of coffee, but it had done nothing to help keep him awake. Exhaustion brought on by boredom still made it a fight to keep from leaning over onto the comm. console in front of him, putting his head on his arms, and just taking a nap. Dustin knew the colonel and Chief Rigger would come up with a very imaginative punishment for him if he did, and he had no desire to find out just how creative the two of them could be if they put their heads together. Rubbing his jaws with the fingers of his right hand as he stifled a yawn, Dustin took a look at the console's screens. Several showed the empty work areas of the Cavern and he ignored those. The only screens that mattered right now were the camera feeds from Larson and Author's suits. The two of them were on the platform near the kaiju corpse's mouth. Both of them were fully geared up and about to enter the kaiju. They were far from the first to enter the kaiju's body via its mouth. The two men had orders from Dr. Hall to get inside the beast tonight and collect some new internal tissues samples so that they would be ready and in her lab when she returned to work herself in the morning. Dustin was glad he was a systems tech and not one of them. The thought of entering the giant monster's corpse through its mouth and climbing down the thing's throat into its body utterly gave him the creeps. He had no idea how guys like Larson and Author did it. One trip into that thing and he was sure he would be flown back to the States and locked up in an asylum for the rest of his life.

In addition to their camera feeds, Dustin had readouts on their suits' systems as well. All his lights were green. He opened a channel to the two men.

"You guys ready out there?" Dustin asked.

"We've just been waiting on you," Larson snorted. "What did you do, take a nap or something? We've been standing around up here for nearly ten minutes waiting on you."

"I wish," Dustin grumbled. "I was just making sure everything is good to go."

"Right," Author chuckled. "I bet you were."

"Oh, come on," Dustin gripped. "We've got all night to get this done."

"Says you," Larson complained. "The sooner this is over with the better."

"What, do you have a hot date or something?" Author teased him.

"Okay, I think we've had enough fun," Dustin told them, forcing himself to be more awake by sheer strength of will. "Let's get this show on the road."

"Roger that," Author answered.

"We're proceeding into the kaiju now," Larson said as the image from his suit's camera shook on Dustin's screen as he got moving.

"How deep are we going tonight?" Author asked.

"Dr. Hall wants a sample from the thing's stomach this time," Dustin reminded them over the comm.

"Dang," Author replied with a sigh. "That'll be the deepest anyone has been into his bad boy yet."

"Who said this thing was a boy?" Larson pointed out. "Do the eggheads know if it even has a gender yet?"

"More moving, less talking," Dustin chimed in. "If you guys want this over with, then pick up the pace already."

"Like you have any right to talk," Larson said snidely.

"I'm working now," Dustin pointed out. "You need to be too."

"You heard the man," Author said, shoving Larson ahead of him into the kaiju's mouth.

There was plenty of room for both of them despite the bulk of their suits. Dustin watched the feed from their suits, staring at the images of the kaiju's teeth surrounding the two men. There were several rows of the teeth, each behind the other, in a circle that filled the edge of the kaiju's mouth. Each tooth was as large as either of the men. Dustin had never gotten used to the size of the thing's teeth, no matter how many jobs like this one he oversaw from the safety of the control room. The size of the kaiju was just as disturbing, if not more so, than what it was.

"You guys be careful in there," Dustin cautioned Larson and Author as they began their descent of the kaiju's throat.

"It would be nice if it didn't smell so bad. You can smell the funk in here even through these suits. It's like someone farted on a sulfur grenade mixed a container of bleach." A gagging sound came over the comm from Author's suit.

"And it only gets worse the more the kaiju thaws out," Larson added.

Dustin went to work running his routine scans of the kaiju's thawing progression as Larson and Author continued their way through its throat. He noticed that sections H through J were reading as warmer than they were supposed to be.

"Larson," Dustin called over the comm. "I'm getting some pretty strange readings coming from the kaiju's abdominal area."

"What kind of readings?" Larson asked.

"They're reading as warmer than they are supposed to be. There aren't any heating units that far down yet though, right?" Dustin asked.

On the feed from Larson suit camera, he saw the motion from Larson shaking his head as the man answered. "No. There aren't. Could be something wrong with the exterior heaters causing the rise in temperatures in those sections. We can take a look once we've got the samples Dr. Hall wants and we get out of here if you want."

"Thanks," Dustin said. "I am going to hold you to that."

Dustin saw both men come to stop in their climb downward inside the kaiju's throat.

"What in the devil?" he heard Author ask Larson. "Did you feel that?"

"Yeah," Larson answered. "It felt like something moving below us."

"It could be kaiju's body shifting," Dustin offered over the comm. "That happens, you know?"

"It does," Author said. "We've both felt that sort of thing before, Dustin. This was something different."

"He's right," Larson confirmed. "This felt more as if there's something in here with us moving around."

"That's impossible." Dustin's eyes were flitting from screen to screen, trying to see if he could spot anything that might be the cause of the movement the two men had felt. The kaiju's body shifting in the ever so slowly melting ice was the most likely cause but... He couldn't find any real sign that it was happening right now. "I think you guys are just getting spooked in there."

"There!" Author exclaimed. "I felt it again."

"Me too," Larson said, confirming the second occurrence of the supposed movement. "Something weird is definitely going on in here."

"I think we should postpone getting those samples that Dr. Hall wants until we know what's going on and that kaiju's corpse is stable," Author suggested.

"Are you kidding?" Larson said. "Maybe you haven't seen her angry before but I have, and it's not something I ever want to experience again."

"I have to agree with Author," Dustin admitted. "And it's my call to make, so I say both of you get the heck out of there until we know more."

"No argument from me," Author assured him.

After a second had passed, Larson's voice rang out breaking the sudden silence. "Okay, Dustin, you're the boss after all. We're headed back up right now."

Dustin waited impatiently on the two men to exit the kaiju's corpse. In all the months they had been studying it, nothing like this had ever happened before. Sure, the corpse had shifted in the ice from time to time as more of it became exposed, and Dr. Hall had warned that the corpse's internal organs could shift inside of it as well, but both men swore it wasn't that this time. They swore it was something else, and that worried Dustin. He didn't like things he couldn't explain. Beyond the shifting of the corpse or that of its organs, there was no other rational explanation for what Larson and Author claimed they had experienced. Dustin had already called Lieutenant Garner to report the anomalous disturbance and the lieutenant was supposed to be on his way. Drumming his fingertips on the console in front of him, Dustin waited with bated breath for Larson and Author to emerge from the kaiju's corpse. Dustin couldn't bear to watch the camera feeds as the two men hurriedly climbed. The jostling of the images was making him motion sick. Instead, he shifted in his seat and took a long look at the sensor data in regards to the position of the kaiju corpse. He figured that would be the first thing the lieutenant asked about when he told him what had happened. Dustin frowned as he confirmed that the kaiju corpse's position hadn't changed from the continued thawing and settling of the body and the ice around it.

The door to the control room opened behind him. Dustin spun his chair around to see a frantic Lieutenant Garner. The lieutenant had to have been asleep when Dustin had called him. His hair was mussed and the shirt of his uniform not fully tucked into his pants. His eyes were sharp and alert though.

"This had better be good, Dustin," Lieutenant Garner warned him.

"Sir, there has been some kind of unexplained movement inside the kaiju corpse. Larson and Author went into the creature's body in order to retrieve more samples for Dr. Hall's work and while they were in its throat…" Dustin was trying to explain when Lieutenant Garner stopped him pointedly.

"That's all you called me for?" Lieutenant Garner snarled at him. "We both know it had just been the shifting of the corpse."

"But it wasn't, sir," Dustin insisted. "The corpse hasn't shifted so much as an inch in the ice."

Lieutenant Garner stared at him in disbelief. "Check your readings again," he ordered.

Dustin ran the check again with Lieutenant Garner watching him over his shoulder. As the results of the check once again confirmed the kaiju corpse's exact position in the ice, Larson's voice echoed in the control room. Both Dustin and the lieutenant jumped at the sound of it. Dustin had left the comm on speaker.

"We're clear," Larson reported. "Empty-handed but clear."

"Roger that," Lieutenant Garner answered before Dustin had the chance to. "Stand down and remain where you are until instructed otherwise."

Dustin caught the quiet huff that Larson gave but nonetheless, Author answered. "Will do, sir, we read you loud and clear."

"Dr. Hall said that there could be shifting of the kaiju's organs and tissues inside its body as well that the exterior sensors wouldn't pick up," Lieutenant Garner commented.

"Sir, with all due respect, that ain't what we felt," Author said through the comm of his suit. "Dustin already suggested that might have been what we experienced but =..."

"It wasn't," Larson spoke up. "Whatever we felt, well, to tell the truth, it was like something below was trying to make its way up the throat towards us."

"That's not only impossible Larson but insane," Lieutenant Garner barked. "You two are the only two people anywhere near that corpse right now. Hades, man, you two are the only people in the entire Cavern at the moment."

"I know what I felt, sir," Larson said, standing his ground. "I never said I could explain it."

Lieutenant Garner gave a Dustin long, hard look then leaned over to mute the comm. "Either of these two on the watch list for psych issues?"

Dustin shook his head. "No, sir," he answered quickly. "In fact, those two are the best two we've got for going inside that thing."

"Holy..." Lieutenant Garner and Dustin both heard Author suddenly shout. "We've got more movement from inside the throat! Something is really moving about in there!"

Dustin could see Lieutenant Garner struggling with what move he should make next then in an instant, the lieutenant decided. "Dustin, get Cavern security in there now!"

As Dustin placed the call, Lieutenant Garner moved to where he could get a clear look through the control room's window at the platform Larson and Author were on. "Tell those two get off that platform and away from the kaiju's mouth."

Dustin unmuted their side of the comlink. "The LT says to get clear of the thing's mouth ASAP! Cavern security is on the way to take over."

"Hold up," Larson shouted. "Whatever was moving in there has stopped. I think whatever was happening might be over."

"I don't care," Lieutenant Garner growled. "Get off that platform or I'll have my men remove you when they arrive."

Already two, heavily armed security troopers were sprinting across the Cavern floor towards the platform. Both of them had drawn their pistols and had them in hand in case of trouble. They reached the ladder at the bottom of the platform as Larson and Author were making their way down it. They had to wait for the two workers to clear it before they could start up it.

"This is all crazy," Dustin heard Lieutenant Garner muttering.

"Like it or not, sir, I think it's time we woke up the colonel. Dr. Hall too," he said. "This is getting out of hand."

Lieutenant Garner nodded at his suggestion. "Do it," he agreed.

The colonel, Dr. Hall, Agent Markson, and the new guy were all in the control in less than ten minutes. Dustin still sat at his console while Lieutenant Garner stood at the back of the room, looking sick. Lieutenant Garner had sent Larson and Author on to run through a quick decontamination but the two security troopers remained in place on the platform at the kaiju's mouth.

"Tell me everything that's happened," Colonel Pitt ordered Dustin and again, he retold the entire series of events.

"It just doesn't make any sense," Dr. Hall said when he was done.

"Exactly," Dustin said, risking her anger.

****

Sam stood with the others in the control room, trying to make sense of what had happened. "And you've never experienced anything like this before?" he asked.

"I've got this, Sam," Dr. Hall snapped at him.

"It doesn't seem that you do, Dr. Hall," Colonel Pitt told her. "Dr. Jessi, if you have an idea about what may be happening here…"

Sam sighed and shook his head. "I don't, sir. Not yet anyway."

Colonel Pitt had ordered Dustin to set open a channel to the two security troopers now standing guard at the mouth of the kaiju corpse. "Hatch, Gregory, any further movement from inside that thing?"

"Negative, sir," Hatch reported in. "Whatever those other two guys were seeing, it's not happening now. It's been calm since we made it up here."

"You're to stay on site until you are relieved," Colonel Pitt ordered.

"Yes, sir," Hatch answered glumly.

"Dustin," Colonel Pitt said, whirling about on the tech, "I want to know that corpse moves so much as a millimeter. Do I make myself clear?"

Dustin swallowed hard and nodded. "Sure thing, Colonel. Count on it."

"As to you two," Colonel Pitt's gaze shifted to fall on Sam and Dr. Hall, "there had better be some answers about what's happened forthcoming in the near future. You have six hours until I send some of *my* men into that thing to find out what's moving down there my way."

"Six hours isn't…" Dr. Hall started, but the angry glare Colonel Pitt shot her caused her to leave her sentence unfinished.

"Six hours," Colonel Pitt told them all again then turned and left the control room.

"Ashley…" Sam said, but she wasn't about to give him the chance to speak.

"I told you, Sam, I don't need your help," Dr. Hall snapped and gestured at the control room's door, indicating to him that his presence wasn't needed. "Now, if you'll excuse me, I have work to do."

"Come on, Sam," Agent Markson urged him. "Let her do this her way and you do it yours."

Sam followed Agent Markson out of the control room. Once they were clear of it, Agent Markson added, "You know she can be a touch temperamental, Sam. I haven't known her as long as you have, but I know she's the best at what she does too."

"She is," Sam agreed. There was no denying how gifted of a scientist Ashley was. In terms of the hard science, he couldn't hold a candle to her on his best day. But then, he had his own means of finding things out.

"I'm headed back to my quarters," Sam told Agent Markson. "No offense, but I work better alone."

"Fine with me," Agent Markson said, laughing. "It's four in the morning. I think I'll catch a few more hours of sleep before the crap really hits the fan if the two of you don't come up with an explanation to the colonel's liking."

"Don't blame you." Sam flashed Agent Markson a grin. "Catch you in a few hours then."

Sam had been in the mess hall when everything went down. He'd had the foresight to stuff an energy drink into the pocket of his pants before he had left it to answer Dustin's call and meet the others in the control room. He was thankful for it now as he walked into his quarters and turned the lights in it up to full. Sam popped open the can, chugging a fourth of it as he eased in the chair at the room's desk and powered up his laptop again. He interlocked his fingers and popped his knuckles before getting to work. As he did, it hit him out of the blue exactly what the movement inside the kaiju was. Sam felt like an idiot for not realizing it at once and cursed himself for a fool. He knocked over the energy drink he'd place on the desk as he leaped to his feet. The can clattered onto the metal floor of his quarters, spilling out its contents. He tripped over it as he started for the door. With a yelp of utter horror, Sam's feet slipped from beneath him and he went crashing down beside the desk. Its corner caught his temple as he fell. Flashes like flicking stars danced in his vision before it went entirely black.

****

Ashley paced about her lab. Dr. Daniel Pressley sat at one of the lab's workstations, looking as stressed out as she was.

"Do you really have to do that?" Dr. Pressley asked.

"It helps me think," Ashley said, coming to a sudden stop. "Did you look at the data I sent to you?"

"I did," Dr. Pressley answered. "Dustin's spot on with his claim that the kaiju didn't shift any. Whatever caused the movement, it didn't have anything to do with the ice that's supporting the bulk of the corpse's weight."

"What could we have missed, Dan?" Ashley said, frowning. "I know Larson and Author. They can be slackers at times but neither of them are easily spooked and they're certainly not liars."

"I listened to the recording of it all," Dr. Pressley told her. "The control room's system automatically records everything that comes over the comms."

"Tell me something I don't know." Ashley's eyes shot dagger at him.

"Well, those two workers mentioned the smell inside the kaiju corpse. We both know it's nasty in there and getting worse every day as the thing continues to thaw. I took a look at their suits. They didn't have any leaks, but there's still a chance from the atmosphere in there got through to them," Dr. Pressley suggested.

"That's possible," Ashley agreed. "I hadn't thought of that."

She knew they were grasping at straws to come up with a rational explanation but…any port in a storm.

"I'll call Dr. Gallenger and have him check out those guys," Dr. Pressley said, proud of himself for coming up with the idea.

"Couldn't hurt," Ashley said with a sigh. "And it is certainly possible, but I don't know that I completely buy it. They weren't in the corpse long, so whatever they were exposed to, if that's truly what occurred, had to be not only strong enough to get through their suits but fast acting too. The two security goons the colonel stationed at the corpse's mouth as guards haven't shown any signs that would give us concern about them. If there was something in the kaiju's throat, logic would dictate that it work eventually bleed out into the Cavern's air."

Dr. Pressley frowned. "There doesn't seem to be any other rational explanation, Ashley. The kaiju has been frozen for millennia. It would be impossible for there to be anything inside it that hasn't gotten in there since the military and private corporations who are funding all this started their work here. There is no chance that something slipped through the base and got into it. And we haven't lost any workers inside the corpse either. I'd certainly remember the paperwork from that if had happened."

Pausing for a moment to think, Dr. Pressley then continued. "There is one other possibility, but you're not going to like it."

Ashley stared at Dr. Pressley. He was a little man with a receding hairline and a pot belly. His wire-rimmed glasses made him look all the more the science nerd that he was.

"And what would that be?" Ashley asked carefully.

"Your friend, what's his name?"

"Sam?" Ashley asked.

"Yeah, this Sam guy. He's new here and desperate to show the colonel that he belongs here. What if he did something to the corpse?" Dr. Pressley matched her stare, meeting her eyes with his own.

"Sam's a lot of things, Dan, but he wouldn't do anything like what you're suggesting. Kaiju are his life. He would be more likely to take his own life than do anything to endanger the validity of a specimen like the one in the Cavern," Ashley answered. "His dream is to show the world that kaiju are real. Messing with that corpse..." she shook her head. "If someone did do something to the kaiju's corpse, it wasn't him."

Dr. Pressley reached over and picked up the mug of coffee sitting on the workstation near him. He took a long sip from it. "Then I got nothing unless my theory about the gases inside the kaiju effecting Larson and Author pans out."

****

Gregory leaned against the platform's railing as Hatch squatted in front of the kaiju corpse's open mouth, peering into it. It was still about another hour until the Cavern would be filled with the workers again. Normally, there were workers in the Cavern around the clock, but Chief Rigger had given the night shift of his crew a well-deserved evening off. As thus, Gregory and Hatch were the only two around and they were far above the Cavern's floor.

"Remind me how we got stuck guarding this thing? This really sucks. We were supposed to be off duty two hours ago," Gregory complained.

Without looking over at Gregory, Hatch shrugged. "Wrong place, wrong time. It's as simple as that, buddy."

"I wonder who got stuck with our real job?" Gregory asked.

"Shawn and Peters were slated to take over for us this morning," Hatch reminded him. "Likely the colonel just added a few hours to their shift and got them up early."

"I'd rather be down there on patrol than up here," Gregory said sincerely. "I'm not a fan of heights."

Hatch laughed. "You're standing a few feet from the body of a real life giant monsters and being on this platform is what you're afraid of?"

Gregory glared at him. "That thing is dead, Hatch. It's been dead a long, long time. A fall from up here though … It's going to get you some broken bones at the very least if you don't snap your neck or spine when you hit that floor down there."

Hatch shook his head. "You're not going to fall, Gregory, unless you do something really stupid. Come on, man."

A hissing noise rose from the depths of the kaiju corpse's throat.

"What in the devil is that?" Gregory asked, coming more alert and leaving his spot at the platform's railing to move closer to Hatch near the corpse's mouth.

"No idea," Hatch admitted, rising to his feet and backing up. He nearly collided with Gregory as the man was moving forward.

"Hey!" Gregory shouted at him. "Watch it. I don't need you pushing me over the side of this thing."

"Sorry," Hatch mumbled before calling for Dustin through his radio. Like them, the tech had been forced to remain on duty. "Dustin, did you pick that noise up over there?"

Dustin's voice came loud and clear through Hatch's handheld radio. "No idea what you're talking about, Hatch. Is something going on over there?"

"Yeah, you could say that," Hatch replied. "We've got a noise coming out of the kaiju's throat. It's like some kind of hissing sound. Do you think it's gas or something being pushed up out of the corpse?"

"Could be. Odds are, it's not dangerous though," Dustin's voice answered. "I advise not breathing it. I'll give Dr. Hall a call and see what she thinks of the situation. In the meantime, hang tight."

Hatch couldn't help but wonder if Dustin was lying to them about the chances of the gas being dangerous. The tech knew as well as they did they were under orders to stay near the corpse's mouth until they were relieved, so even if it was dangerous, they weren't going anywhere until someone showed up to take their place.

"That's just great that is," Gregory scowled.

"If it's escaping gas making that noise, it's odorless," Hatch said.

"Those are the worst kind," Gregory said, though he really had no idea what he talking about. He was a soldier not a biologist, but he had stories about Egyptian tombs and the like where pent-up gases could be lethal when they were released and breathed in.

"Holy crap," Hatch shouted, taking another step back to stand side by side with Gregory. "Did you see that?"

"What?" Gregory asked.

"Something moved in there," Hatch told him pointing at the rear of the kaiju corpse's mouth.

"You're crazy, man," Gregory said, but then he saw it too. There was something moving just out of their line of sight in the shadows back there.

"Dustin," Hatch called over the radio. "We've got movement in the kaiju."

Both Hatch and Gregory drew their pistols without waiting on Dustin to reply.

"Say again," Dustin urged them. "I didn't copy that."

Hatch's heart skipped a beat as he saw the thing rising up out of the kaiju's throat. The yellow fires of its eyes glowed in the shadows of the kaiju's mouth. It finished its climb and stood up to its full height. The creature only stood a bit over five feet tall, but nonetheless, it was menacing. It wore no clothes. Thick scales covered its body from head to toe. Each of its feet ended in three-pronged appendages from which extended blade-like talons. It had the shape of a man though its arms were longer and closer to resembling those of an ape. Its hands were five fingered like a human, but they too ended in razor-like claws that gleamed in the light spilling into the kaiju corpse's mouth from the Cavern outside it. The hissing noise was coming from it as it sucked in breath through its overly large mouth and rows of glistening, razor-like teeth. A forked tail protruded from its back. Its spiked tips rose up over the creature's shoulder blades and flicked about in the air above it.

Hatch and the creature stared at each other. He had no idea what the creature was waiting on but he, despite all the combat he had seen over the years, was frozen with shock. An abomination like the thing in front of him had no right to exist in the real world. He knew it was a predator and he was about to be its prey but still, he couldn't bring his body to move.

The sharp crack of a 9mm pistol firing snapped Hatch into motion. He threw himself flat to make sure he was clear of Gregory's line of fire. Gregory's pistol cracked three times in rapid succession. Hatch watched as the rounds struck the creature's scale-covered form and sparked off of it to embed themselves in the softer, decaying flesh of the interior of the kaiju corpse's mouth. The creature looked down at its body as if checking to see if it had been injured and then raised it head in Gregory's direction. Its hiss turned into a mighty roar as it lunged forward with impossible speed. Streaking by Hatch where he lay, it plowed into Gregory, knocking his pistol from his grasp with an almost supernatural ease. The pistol went flying through the air to clatter onto the floor of the Cavern far below the platform the three of them were on. A swipe from the creature's other hand opened up Gregory's abdomen in a single fluid motion. Gregory's guts exploded out of him, red-slicked, purple strands of intestines sliding free of the body that had housed them. Gregory screamed in pain. It echoed in the Cavern as Gregory grabbed at his loose guts, trying to force them back inside of him. The creature's claws flashed again, reducing Gregory's throat to a mass of mangled and torn flesh. Hatch scrambled to his feet as Gregory's dead body toppled over the side of the platform to splatter the floor below with his blood and entrails.

Yanking his pistol free of its holster, Hatch leveled it at the creature as it turned towards him. There was a deep hunger in its eyes. Out of instinct and training more than conscious effort, Hatch took aim at the creature and pulled the pistol's trigger. The bullet that left the barrel of his gun was too slow to strike the creature. It sidestepped the incoming round, almost a blur as it moved, having seen what a weapon like the one Hatch had fired at it could do.

Hatch could hear Dustin yelling at him over the radio he had dropped. He ignored the radio and the tech's frantic cries, his attention focused entirely on living through the next few minutes. Taking aim at the creature again as it strolled leisurely towards him like a cat toying with its food, he loosed a trio of shots at it. The creature was fast enough to dodge the first, but the other two struck it this time. One caught the creature in its shoulder. Though the bullet bounced away harmlessly, its impact did give the creature pause. The second slammed into its forehead a fraction of a second later. The second round's impact jerked the creature's head back atop its neck. The creature seemed stunned. Hatch used the moment to keep pouring bullets into it. More rounds sparked away from its scales as the creature shook its head as if to clear it and then snarled its displeasure at him. It lunged forward at him like a springing cat, though much faster than any cat could ever hope to be. Only luck saved Hatch's life. As he turned to try and dodge, one of his feet slipped from beneath him and he fell out of the path of the creature's leap. It disappeared over the side of the platform behind him.

Hatch could hear gunfire from beneath the platform and knew that Shawn and Peters must have rushed into the Cavern from their post at the sound of the gunfire. Racing to the edge of the platform, he rammed into the railing there, barely able to catch himself in time not to go following after the creature into the Cavern below. He saw Shawn and Peters. Hatch figured his two fellow soldiers didn't stand a snowball's chance in hell of stopping the creature. Peters' rifle blazed away on full auto at the creature where it had landed nimbly on its feet and crouched, ready to spring again. Bullets hammered into the Cavern's floor where the thing had been as it leaped once more. Shawn tried to bring his rifle up in time to get a burst off at the creature, but its scale-covered body came crashing on top of him before he managed to. Claws flashed and blood sprayed as it ripped apart Shawn's chest and shoulders in a series of insanely fast slashes before it leaped again. Its flight carried it to the Cavern's entrance where its three-toed feet thudded onto the metal floor there. Peters spun about, tracking the creature with the barrel of his rifle and keeping his finger on the weapon's trigger. He caught the creature with a stream of fully automatic fire that sent it staggering. The higher-powered rounds of Shawn's rifle penetrated the creature's scales. Black blood erupted in a series of mini explosions from where the rounds from Shawn's rifle dug into its body. The creature turned to glance at him, roaring its fury at Shawn as if promising him a gory and unimaginable death, then dashed through the doorway leading out of the Cavern. Dustin had to be watching everything that was happening because those doors were already in the process of closing as the creature moved through them. They clanged shut loudly in the creature's wake.

Mouth hanging open and amazed that he was still alive and breathing, Hatch released his white-knuckled hold on the platform's railing and sprinted over to the ladder leading down from it. The creature was like a nightmare come to life and it was now loose in Alpha Station.

God help whoever it comes across next, Hatch thought as he climbed down as fast he could.

****

Agent Markson wasn't usually the type to let exhaustion get to him. This morning, he was really feeling it though. His eyes were bloodshot and his always perfect suit, not so perfect. The night had been an odd one. He'd been awakened in the wee hours because of a disturbance involving the kaiju corpse. Whatever was going on with the dead monster, he had no idea what it was. It didn't seem to be dangerous as far as anyone could tell yet though. Nonetheless, Agent Markson was glad that Colonel Pitt assigned men to keep a closer watch on the gigantic body.

After walking Dr. Jessi to his quarters the emergency meeting in the Cavern's control room was concluded, Agent Markson planned on getting in a couple hours of sleep. That hadn't panned out from him though. Agent Markson made a grievous miscalculation about how long it would take to report the disturbance to his superiors back home. Even with the help of the topside comm officer on the surface above Alpha Station and over an hour of efforts made in vain, there was just no getting a signal out. The storm that rolled in above the subterranean complex was just creating too much interference with the comm gear. He supposed he could have tried his personal satellite phone, but that meant bundling up, donning a parka, and going out into the storm to try to use it. Since the disturbance appeared to be over with and things seemed to be in hand, Agent Markson went to the mess hall instead after his failed attempt. The morning shift workers were just beginning to show up in the mess and the large room smelled of eggs and pancake syrup. Thankfully, the disturbance had occurred on a night that Chief Rigger had let them have some much-needed rest from their normal around the clock time table or things might have gotten out of hand. At this point, only a handful of the residents of Alpha Station knew about the disturbance at all. That would change quickly though and he knew it. It didn't really matter, but Agent Markson was used to keeping secrets and putting a proper spin on information before it went out to the masses.

Not sticking around to converse with morning's work crew, Agent Markson snagged a cup of black coffee and strolled through Alpha Station's corridors at a laid back pace. He was surprised that Dr. Hall or Sam hadn't come up with an answer to it all yet. If they had, he knew he would have surely heard about it already.

As he approached the entrance to the Cavern, sipping at his much-needed coffee, he heard the sound of gunfire coming from around the bend in the corridor ahead of him. *What in the bloody Hades?* Agent Markson thought as he tossed his cup of coffee aside and drew the pistol holstered on his hip.

That was when he saw the creature. It came scrambling along the side of the corridor wall around the bend ahead of him. It was literally racing across the wall, the sharp claws of its hands digging into their metal as it moved. The thing's eyes burned a feral yellow that caused a shiver to run down his spine as he took aim at it. It apparently noticed him as well because it unleashed a fearsome roar that echoed in the enclosed space of the corridor around Agent Markson.

He didn't know what it was, but he was dang sure it needed to die. Agent Markson squeezed his pistol's trigger, putting a cluster of shots into the thing's face and head. Some of the shots pinged harmlessly away, bouncing off the scales that covered its entire body. One though struck the creature in its mouth, shattering several of the razor-like teeth. The monster, or whatever it was, toppled from the wall to the corridor's floor, spitting what appeared to be globs of black blood from its mouth. Agent Markson pressed his momentary advantage, running towards the creature while it was writhing about, emptying his pistol's magazine into it as he ran. Shot after shot sparked against the creature's scaled body but with no other discernable effect. Agent Markson popped the weapon's spent magazine, discarding it, and slamming another one home as the creature lifted itself to its feet. It was an inch or so shorter than he was. That didn't make the thing any less lethal though and he knew it.

Agent Markson noticed the creature was bleeding from wounds on its left side and back. They leaked the same black blood that dangled in strands from the creature's mouth where his first shot had knocked out some of its teeth. Someone had managed to hurt it before it escaped the Cavern before the large area could be locked down. The closing of the Cavern's bulkhead-like doors must have been the sound he heard in the seconds prior to the creature coming into view. All of his other previous shots at the creature had failed to hurt it except for the lucky one to the thing's mouth. Agent Markson aimed his next burst of shots at the wounds on the creature's side. The creature rolled as he fired, bringing its uninjured chest around to take the brunt of his fire. As the creature rolled, its tail lashed out at Agent Markson. It would have taken his head from his shoulders in a shower of blood had one of his bullets not found its target while the creature was still in the process of rolling over. The creature shrieked an inhuman cry of pain as the bullet pierced its already injured left side, digging into its internal tissues there. The jerk the creature gave twisted the arc of its tail through the air at Agent Markson just enough that it only slashed a small line of red across his neck. Agent Markson slapped a hand over the bleeding cut on his neck as he staggered backwards away from the thrashing creature.

Agent Markson stumbled into the corridor's wall, using it to brace himself. The wound on his neck wasn't much more than a flesh wound but he knew his system was in shock. The world spun before his eyes as he fought to regain his senses and balance. He could hear the creature's continued wails as it tried in vain to reach into its own side and tear out the bullet there. Seeing that its efforts were only causing itself more pain, the creature righted itself, standing up to face him again. Agent Markson raised the barrel of his pistol towards the thing and started emptying what was left of his second magazine at it. It was his last and his only hope of keeping the thing at bay. Spent rounds flew from the gun's side as they were ejected from it. They clattered to the corridor floor at his feet. The creature stood there for a moment, allowing the bullets to ricochet from its scales, staring at him. Markson figured he was dead as the creature started moving, but instead of coming at him, it whirled about and ripped the cover from a nearby ventilation shaft, diving into it.

Swallowing hard, Agent Markson stared at the effortlessly tossed aside cover of the heating vent. The cover had been bolted in place. Those bolts lay in shattered pieces near the bent metal of the vent cover itself. *Just how strong is that thing?* he wondered. As it truly sunk in that he was alive and the creature was gone from the corridor, Agent Markson threw himself into motion. He tore a piece of his shirt, tying it about his neck as a makeshift bandage, as he ran to the closest comm panel in Alpha Station's corridor system that he remembered the location of. It was right next to the massive, sealed doors of the Cavern. He stabbed it with the tip of his pointer finger.

"Dustin!" he yelled, knowing the tech was either still manning the Cavern's control room or dead.

"Little busy right now, Agent Markson!" Dustin's panic stricken voice answered him. "We've got folks dead in here!"

"The creature!" Agent Markson shouted at the tech. "It's in the heating vents!"

He knew Dustin heard him because alarm klaxons began to blare throughout all of Alpha Station.

****

Chief Rigger sat across from Perry and Amanda at the table they were sharing in the mess. The mess was fairly crowded for how early it was. That surprised Chief Rigger. He thought a lot more of his work crew would be in bed, sleeping off all the drinking they had surely done in the down time he gave them the night before. The fact that they weren't spoke volumes about just what a spectacular crew they were. He was on his second plate of eggs, pancakes, and syrup-smothered bacon when the alarm klaxons began to blare. Perry and Amanda looked at him with frightened expressions at the sound of them, waiting on him to tell them what to do.

"You don't think it's the power station, do you, Chief?" Perry asked. The man was convinced that one day the generators were going to blow beyond repair and that they were all going to freeze to death before help could reach them. Chief Rigger supposed there were worse things to be afraid of, and normally he didn't mind Perry's craziness, but right now he wanted to punch the man in his face. Of course it wasn't the power station or the lights would be out or at least flickering.

A voice came over the radio on his belt making Chief Rigger flinch. He jerked the radio from his belt, half-cursing, half-praising himself for forgetting to turn it off. "Rigger here," he answered.

"Chief!" Dustin's voice was almost trembling as he spoke. "We've got a problem. Something, we don't know what exactly, crawled out of the kaiju corpse. It's already killed two of Colonel Pitt's men and according to Agent Markson, it's gotten into Alpha Station's heating vents."

"Blessed mother," Chief Rigger muttered. "Can you tell me what it is?"

"Negative on that," Dustin answered. "The colonel is scrambling all his men to track the thing and kill it, but since it's in the heating vents …"

"You called me," Chief Rigger finished for him.

"Right," Dustin agreed. "We thought you might have some ideas on where the thing would go."

Chief Rigger and everyone else in the mess looked up as *something* loudly thudded through the heating vents above them.

"You could say that," the chief answered but didn't have time to say anything more before the ceiling over the mess where the vent ran came crashing downward. In the spray of splinters, metal shards, and other debris, a creature straight out of a nightmare dropped onto the mess's floor. It looked about the large room with blazing yellow eyes. A two-pronged tail slashed through the air behind its body.

"Everybody out!" Chief Rigger screamed.

A worker with the bad luck to be standing where the creature had dropped into the mess lost the right side of his face to a swipe of the thing's claws. The blow not only ripped away his nose and mangled his right cheek, but it sent him flying several feet across the mess. His body hit the floor with a loud thud and the sound of snapping bone.

Another worker leaped at the creature, swinging her metal food tray at it. The creature moved under the tray she swung it and came up in front of her, ripping her open from groin to throat. Blood splattered everywhere.

There were two of Colonel Pitt's men in the mess. They had drawn their pistols and were shouting for folks to get out of their line of fire. The mess sunk into utter chaos as some fled for the door, others hit the floor trying to crawl under the tables, and a few stood their ground. Chief Rigger was among the later. He didn't have a real weapon with him, but he had geared up before coming to breakfast so that he would be able to go straight to work afterwards. A huge wrench he was planning on using on some of Alpha Station's piping leaned against the table where he had been sitting. He snatched it up into his hands as the two soldiers opened fire on the monster. The sound of their pistols being fired rang out amid the screams of those trying to avoid the creature. The bullets hit the creature's scale-covered body, knocking it backwards but didn't appear to have any more of an effect on it beyond that. The monster recovered with impossible speed. It lifted a table over its head and hurled it at the two soldiers. One of them managed to throw himself from the table's path. A bullet from the other soldier's gun splintered the center of the table right before it hit him. The table's weight crushed the soldier against the wall behind him. It was thrown with enough force that when it pinned him against the wall, a geyser of blood erupted from his mouth as his ribs caved inward.

The creature sprung up onto the top of the nearest table and began leaping from one table to the next across the mess. The remaining soldier saw it coming at him. Jerking the barrel of his pistol up in the monster's direction, he was able to put three rounds into its chest before it reached him. The shots didn't even slow the thing down this time. It kept coming like a runaway freight train. The soldier turned to run. The monster's powerful legs hurled it from the last of the tables between it and its prey. It landed on the soldier's back, catching the sides of his head with its clawed hands. Those claws sunk into the man's flesh, digging to the bone of his skull, as it firmed up its grip. With a quick and far too easy jerk, it yanked the soldier's head from his shoulders, flinging it towards the mess's kitchen area. The monster had already jumped from the soldier's falling body before it toppled to the floor. The flight of its jump carried it near the mess's main doorway. The slower of the fleeing workers didn't even have time to react as it tore into them. Its hand plunged into one woman's back and re-emerged holding a piece of her spinal column. The man next to her managed to turn toward the creature. What he thought he was going to be able to do, Chief Rigger had not a clue. He watched as the monstrous creature took the piece of the woman's spine that it clutched and drove it into the man's forehead. The bone plunged through the man's skull like a knife blade despite its bluntness. Another testament to just how strong the monster was.

Chief Rigger noticed the monster was bleeding. There were wounds on its back and side from where someone had shot it with something far more powerful than the pistols used by the two soldiers it had just murdered.

Perry and Amanda were still at his side. Neither of them had fled with the others. Amanda's fingers were curled around the bottom of the knife she had been using for her breakfast in a white-knuckled grip. Perry held a hammer from his belt of tools at the ready should the monster notice them and come their way. And it did...

Most everyone else was either dead or been able to escape into the corridor beyond the mess's doorway. The creature sniffed at the air and its head whipped around in their direction.

"Those wounds," Chief Rigger told Perry and Amanda. "That's where we have to hit it if we want to have a prayer of stopping it."

The creature's form almost seemed to blur from its speed as it charged them. Chief Rigger moved to meet it head on, swinging his heavy wrench. The creature was faster than he was though and lashed out shoving him from its path. Chief Rigger went toppling over a table to crash onto the floor behind it as the creature reached Perry. Perry's eyes went wide as one of the creature's clawed hands reached into his abdomen and came out clutching a handful of his guts. Amanda screamed at the top of her lungs as she came around Perry to stab the blade of her knife into one of the masses of torn scales that were leaking black blood on the creature's side. It screeched as if driven mad by the unexpected pain. A backhanded blow knocked Amanda off her feet and sent her bouncing along the mess hall's floor away from it. The creature's hand that had been holding Perry's intestines released the red-slicked strands that stunk to high heavens and plunged back inside of him. The claws of that hand moved upwards inside of Perry as their tips poked through his ribs and came tearing through the cloth of his shirt to glisten under the mess hall's lights. It held Perry in place by his ribs as Perry moaned and weakly struggled to break free of the hand that was inside him. The creature raised its other hand, sticking its pointer and middle fingers into Perry's eyes. They sunk inward all the way to the creature's knuckles as Perry spasmed and thrashed. Perry's body went limp and the creature fluidly and with blinding speed removed its hand from his falling body.

Amanda was back on her feet behind it. She had no weapon now though. The hilt of her knife protruded from the creature's side where she had stuck it. The creature pulled the knife out and licked its own black blood from the blade.

Chief Rigger had scrambled onto his feet as well. He came charging at the creature with his heavy wrench. As the creature turned to engage him, Amanda, either driven mad from the horrors all around her or too brave for her own good, dove at the creature. Her flailing, outstretched hands managed to grab its arms. She wasn't strong enough to stop the creature's movement but she did slow it just enough for Chief Rigger to carry through with his plan. His heavy wrench arced through the air with all the force he could muster and the weight of his charging body driving it. It smashed into the creature's skull with such force that Chief Rigger felt the aftershocks of the blow vibrating up the lengths of his thick arms. The creature's head was snapped sideways atop its neck with the resounding crack of breaking bone. Even in death, the thing managed one last swipe at him. One of its clawed hands removed the flesh from the side of the chief temple and his left eye along with it as both their bodies smashed onto the mess hall's floor. As he lay on top of the creature's dead body, Chief Rigger's own head lolled sideways as blackness over took him and he lost consciousness.

The last thing Chief Rigger heard before the world faded away was Amanda's strained voice screaming for a medic.

****

Sam came awake with a start, sitting bolt right on the bed he was lying in. A man in the white coat of a medical doctor was standing over him by the bed's side.

"Whoa, take it easy there," the doctor told him. "You've taken quite a hit to the head."

"At least it wasn't somewhere vital to him," Sam heard Ashley quip and noticed her sitting in a chair nearby.

"Where am I?" Sam asked. The world was spinning around him and his skull felt like a professional wrestler had been pounding on it with a sledgehammer.

"You're in Alpha Station medical section, Sam," Ashley explained before the doctor could. "The nice gentlemen taking care of you is Dr. Gallenger."

"We found you on the floors of your quarters," Dr. Gallenger added.

"How long have I been out?" Sam croaked. "And can I please have some water?"

Dr. Gallenger poured him a cup from the pitcher that sat on the table opposite Ashley's chair and handed it to him.

"As to how long you've been out," Dr. Gallenger said, "we can't know for sure, as it took us some time to figure out where you were with everything that's happened. I would estimate around eight hours though but again, that's just a guess."

"What do you mean by everything that's happened?" Sam asked after chugging half the cup.

58

Dr. Gallenger reached to take it away from him. "You need to take things slow right now, okay? You're going to be fine but like I said, that was a pretty nasty bump to your skull that you took."

"Sam…" Ashley started, and he knew from her tone it wasn't going be good news. "During the time you were out, we discovered what was inside the kaiju corpse."

"She was pregnant when she was frozen, Ashley," Sam blurted out. "I don't know how we could have missed realizing that."

Ashley nodded. "You're right, Sam." She made a face as she said the words as if doing so disgusted her.

"I knew it." Sam smiled.

"It's nothing to smile about, Sam," Ashley told him. "The baby kaiju… It climbed up her throat and got loose in Alpha Station. We're still picking up the pieces and getting things sorted out, but we know it killed at least seven people and wounded more before we were able to stop it."

Sam's smile vanished from his lips as he stared at her, not knowing how to respond.

"Colonel Pitt is on the edge of shutting this entire project down. I think he would have already but like the folks paying for it all, he's afraid this might be our only chance to learn all we can about stopping larger kaiju like the mother we have in the Cavern Sam before one of them shows up alive somewhere," Ashley said with a frown, getting up from her chair.

"How did you get him not to do it?" Sam asked, sure that the colonel was going to take some kind of action given.

"We've started picking up some very strange shifts in temperatures in the kaiju's body." Ashley stood over him as her voice took on an even more serious tone. "I've agreed to let the colonel send some of his men, 'packing some real firepower' as he put it, inside her body to make sure there aren't any more surprises waiting for us in there. Honestly, he was going to do it whether I agreed or not. I may be the head of the project in the eyes of the corporations funding it, but he's the one who is really in charge."

"If there was a baby alive inside of her, isn't the colonel concerned she'll wake up too?" Sam moved his pillows around to prop up on them as they talked.

Ashley shook her head. "No. I've run enough tests on the mother kaiju to know that she is really and truly dead. What killed her? I have no idea, but whatever did it, did it fast, and beyond the freezing from the ice, there's no damage to her body or tissues that I have been able to see."

"What about the baby? Do you know how it was able to stay alive inside her all these years?" Sam asked.

"That I have a theory on at least." Ashley actually flashed a sincere grin with no malice or sarcasm for once. "Based on what I have learned about kaiju physiology, I believe that kaiju can enter a state of dormancy and remain that way indefinitely until some other force wakes them up. Think of it as biological stasis. Her baby must have been in such a state at the time of her death or entered it shortly thereafter to preserve itself."

"That would explain a lot," Sam replied. "It also would mean that Colonel Pitt is right to be concerned about there being other larger kaiju like the mother in the Cavern just waiting to be woken up."

"I have to ask, how did you know she was pregnant?" Ashley stared at him as she spoke. "And if you make some joke about being psychic, I will make sure you're never getting up from that bed."

"My research," Sam admitted. "Right before I fell, I came across the legend of the first kaiju. Her name was Quixil. The writings about her are the oldest known kaiju legend I've ever come across in my work. Reading about her and her children got me to thinking. It wasn't difficult to put two and two together from there."

"I'm impressed, Sam," she said, taking his hand. "I really am."

"Thanks," Sam stammered. "Uh... I hate to tell you this, but kaiju mothers don't just have one baby."

Ashley nodded at him. "Yeah, based on those odd temp readings, I figured that one out for myself. Let's just hope the colonel realizes what he's sending his men into. Who knows how many more creatures like the one that tore through this base are inside of her. Regardless, I am working on a means of making sure that if there are any other of those things inside her that they remain in their current state of bio-stasis. I believe they must have gone into a dormant state the mother was frozen before. I doubt he'll give me time for that though. You know how the military is. But, the strange temp readings don't necessarily mean the others are awake, and we had best hope that they aren't."

"I suppose the colonel is hoping to catch them while they're still slumbering," Sam said, chuckling darkly. "He does realize that if his men fail to kill them, they will surely wake them up if they aren't already right?"

"He's military, Sam," Ashley said as if the simple statement explained everything. "His answer to everything is to kill it if it causes problems."

"I think that's enough for now," Dr. Gallenger interrupted them. "Dr. Jessi needs his rest. I'm keeping him overnight for observation. If all goes as I think it will, he'll be released in the morning."

Ashley stopped in the room's doorway on her way out to glance back at him a final time. "Sam..." she started, and he thought for a fleeting instant that she might actually be about to apologize to him for how she had treated him and his work for so many years now. That hope was crushed as she said, "Listen to Dr. Gallenger and take all the time you need. There's not much a cryptozoologist can do to help at this point anyway."

And then she was gone.

****

As Ashley left Sam's left, Dr. Gallenger followed her.

Once they were outside, she asked, "And you're sure Sam is going to be okay?"

Dr. Gallenger nodded. "Yes. He'll be fine. I wish I could say the same for my other patient."

He gestured at the doorway to the only other real patient room in Alpha Station's small medical section.

Ashley knew the room belonged to Chief Rigger. The chief had been the one to end the small kaiju's rampage through the base but at a great cost. In its death throes, the creature had raked his face with its claws. Glancing through the doorway at where the chief lay unconscious, Ashley saw the bandages wrapped around the upper left side of his face and head.

"Just how bad was the chief hurt?" Ashley asked. She had heard about his fight with the small kaiju. It was already growing into something of a legend among Alpha Station's personnel. The chief took the creature out with only a large wrench and the sheer determination to save everyone else that he could. The big man was a hero now.

"Skull fracture," Dr. Gallenger told her. "A bad one too. Any worse and I would have had to ask the colonel to fly him out stateside. Given our current situation, who knows if the colonel would have even permitted it. As it is, I've got it under control, and he's stable by the grace of God."

"The chief's tough," Ashley said, continuing to stare at the big man in the bed through the doorway.

"He's going to be dealing with some big changes in his life when he comes around," Dr. Gallenger sighed. "Losing an eye... It will likely take him some time to re-learn certain parts of his job. His depth perception will be radically different."

"If anyone can adjust, he can," Ashley assured Dr. Gallenger.

"I don't doubt it, but it's still going to be a hard change." Dr. Gallenger's frown matched her own. "Now if you'll excuse me, I've got a lot of work to do. The colonel wants me to be ready when he sends his men into the kaiju corpse. We only have so much space here so I have to adjust too."

"Take care of Sam," Ashley told him and then wandered out into Alpha Station's corridors. She headed back to her lab where she found Dr. Pressley and her assistant, Laura, waiting on her.

"Have you heard?" Dr. Pressley asked almost in a panic.

"Have I heard what?" Ashley moved to her work station, opening her laptop.

"The colonel," Laura said. "He's getting his men prepared to go into the kaiju corpse right now."

"Bloody, freaking idiot," Ashley ragged, slamming her laptop closed, knowing there was no time for her to do anything useful on it. "So much for the time to come up with a means of keeping any more creatures inside the corpse from waking up!"

"I tried to stop him," Laura said, looking sick. "Just like you told me to. He wouldn't listen though."

"I should have known the man wasn't going to give us time to try anything," Ashley said.

"You're not concerned about them damaging our specimen?" Dr. Pressley sipped at the cup of tea he clutched in his hands. Ashley could smell the chamomile from where she stood. Pressley used teas for everything from his health to keep his nerves in line. Today, apparently, he felt he needed a triple dose of chamomile to calm him down.

"I don't think we need to be concerned about that at all," Ashley said. "We've never been able to map the thing's internal structure anyway due to its scales and the EM radiation contained in its tissues blocking everything we've tried. The colonel's mad expedition, well, it will give us the footage from his men's suit cameras to look at."

"And if there are more of those things in the creature, our work here is done anyway," Laura added. "We'll all be running for our lives."

"Let's hope it doesn't come to that," Ashley said. "The helicopters here don't have room for us all, and if more of those things do get woken up and loose, they'll be our only way out."

****

Lieutenant Bellmore, Hatch, and three other soldiers stood geared up and ready to go on the platform that led into the kaiju corpse's mouth. Another twelve heavily armed soldiers waited on the Cavern floor below them. Those men weren't going in like Bellmore and his crew. They were there to make sure anything else that came out of the kaiju corpse was dead before it escaped into Alpha Station. The huge bulkhead doors were closed in preparation for just such an eventuality.

The colonel was in the Cavern's control room with the tech, Dustin, who had been on duty when the first creature emerged. The colonel specifically picked Dustin to be the tech for this operation just as he picked Hatch to be a part of the crew going into the dead beast. Both of them had seen what an infant kaiju could do on an up close and personal level. Lieutenant Bellmore understood the reasoning behind the colonel using the two men as he was, but even so, he wondered if Hatch should really be a part of his crew. He could hear Hatch's breathing over the comm of the hazmat-like suit that he his crew wore. Hatch sounded on the edge of hyperventilating in his.

"You gonna be okay?" Lieutenant Bellmore asked, moving to put a hand on the shoulder of Hatch's suit.

"I'll be fine, sir," Hatch stammered. "I can handle this."

"If you can't, it would be better for us all if you spoke up now," Lieutenant Bellmore urged.

Hatch had watched the creature that had come out of the kaiju kill his watch partner and another soldier before it began its killing spree in Alpha Station. Lieutenant Bellmore knew Hatch had seen men die before. Most of the military personnel assigned to Alpha Station had. But seeing a friend ripped apart by the claws of a monster that resembled something straight out of a horror movie and someone shot on a battlefield were two entirely different things.

Lieutenant Bellmore looked Hatch over a final time, appraising the man, and decided to trust him. Hatch had never let him down before, and he had faith that the soldier's training would kick in and hold him together if they did run into trouble inside the kaiju.

"Lieutenant," Colonel Pitt's voice rang out of the comm. "Status?"

"We're good to go, sir," Lieutenant Bellmore answered.

"Then be about it then," Colonel Pitt ordered.

"Everyone double check comms and suit cams," Lieutenant Bellmore told his men. "We're going in."

The kaiju's throat had been hollowed out to a degree and a ladder had been fixed in place leading into the depths of the creature's body. The ladder only went down so far though and after that, the squad would be using rope to continue their descent.

The lights of the soldiers' suits played over the decaying tissue of the interior of the kaiju's throat as they climbed. Lieutenant Bellmore gagged as the creature's stench hit him even through his suit. He heard others in his squad gagging from the smell of it too. It was like sulfur mixed with rotting meat. Lieutenant Bellmore wondered if creatures like this one breathed fire. Certainly some of the kaiju that Hollywood brought to life on the silver screen did. Could monsters like this one by the basis of the legends about dragons? He hoped not. Lieutenant Bellmore truly prayed this thing was the only one of its kind.

The squad reached the end of the ladder and Striker, the soldier at the bottom, began to ready the rope they would be using to go beyond it.

"Striker," Lieutenant Bellmore called. "You see anything down there?"

"Negative, sir," Striker answered. "Not moving anyway."

Lieutenant Bellmore frowned. "Explain."

"There are marks all over the interior of the kaiju's throat, sir," Striker told him.

"What kind of marks?"

"Claw marks, sir, like more of creatures like the one that came out have been climbing around in here." Striker's voice held an edge of real fear.

"Hold your position," Lieutenant Bellmore ordered.

The five soldiers were spread out along the ladder at intervals of six feet apart. Lieutenant Bellmore was in the group's middle. He wanted to see what Striker was seeing with his own eyes before he made the call on what to do next. That meant climbing around and over Hatch who was between them. Though the kaiju's throat was wide, the darkness and spots of newly frozen ice from where the original ice would melt only to refreeze made it difficult to maneuver. Not being careful could cost one their life and Lieutenant Bellmore knew it. The thin ice on the ladder could be hard to see with just the lights of the squad's suits. Ever so cautiously, he eased himself on, managing to get past Hatch. As he went by, Hatch did his best to move aside for him.

Lieutenant Bellmore reached Striker's position and hung awkwardly beside him on the ladder, staring into the darkness below. The kaiju's throat continued downwards towards its stomach, but even with the light of from his suit, the stomach was still beyond his line of sight. Turning his attention to the sides of the kaiju's throat, he took a look at the reason he had joined Striker. He saw the claw marks the younger man had told him about. The inside of the kaiju's throat had been shredded. It looked like *something* had been crawling over the sides of the throat. More than one something too, based on the severity of the damage to its tissue. Lieutenant Bellmore wasn't an easily spooked man but right now every instinct in him was screaming from him to abort the op and order his squad out of the kaiju's corpse.

"Sir!" Striker suddenly shouted at him.

Lieutenant Bellmore saw that Striker was pointing at something below them. His gaze moved in the direction that the younger man was indicating. His heart skipped a beat inside his chest as he saw the yellow eyes glowing in the darkness below them. At first, it was just one pair but the number quickly grew. Within the passing of only a few seconds, Lieutenant Bellmore found himself staring into a sea of those feral, hungry yellow eyes.

They filled the throat of the kaiju corpse below the bottom of the ladder.

"Sir?" Striker's voice had become a whisper over the comm of his suit.

Lieutenant Bellmore's hand that wasn't keeping a solid grip on the ladder moved to clutch his weapon where it hung from a strap about his shoulder. His finger slid onto its trigger.

"Steady," Lieutenant Bellmore warned Striker. "We don't want to do anything to provoke them."

Striker was silent as he and Lieutenant Bellmore watched the creatures below them. The creatures were holding their position and watching them too. It reminded Lieutenant Bellmore of two gunfighters on the street of some town in the old west, each waiting on the other to draw first.

Lieutenant Bellmore grimaced as Striker shifted ever so slightly on the ladder next to him. That tiny bit of movement was all it took to launch the creatures into motion. They surged upwards, scurrying along the sides of the kaiju corpse's throat.

"Everybody out!" Lieutenant Bellmore shouted as he swung the barrel of his weapon downwards towards the swarming kaiju and squeezed its trigger. The weapon's barrel flashed in the darkness as he sprayed the kaiju with a stream of fully automatic fire.

****

"We've got gunfire inside the kaiju!" Dustin shouted at Colonel Pitt as he spun around in his chair at the console of the Cavern's control room.

"I can hear that, Dustin," Colonel Pitt snapped, watching the live feeds streaming in from the suits of Lieutenant Bellmore's squad.

Though the audio was coming in clear, the video feeds weren't. There was too much interference from the corpse itself. It was hard to see much of anything other than flashes of gunfire and the frantic jostling about of the cameras as Lieutenant Bellmore and his squad started up the ladder towards the kaiju's mouth.

The screens of showing the feeds from Lieutenant Bellmore and Striker's cameras went black.

"Get them out of there!" Colonel Pitt roared at Dustin.

The tech was like a deer caught in the headlights of a fast moving car. It was clear he had no idea how he was supposed to magically get the men inside the kaiju out of it.

"Abort mission!" Dustin cried over the comm. "I say again, abort mission!"

The images from the live feed of Hatch's camera showed his weapon blazing away at something not in the camera's line of sight.

"Die, you mothers! Die!" Hatch was yelling.

The guards stationed on the Cavern floor broke into two groups. Half of them kept their position on the Cavern's floor as the other half hurried up the ladder to the platform that the kaiju corpse's mouth opened onto. Sergeant Bible was the first of them to reach the platform. As soon as he was on it, he pumped a round into the chamber of the heavy shotgun he carried and aimed it at the kaiju's mouth.

The feed from Hatch's camera had gone dark. The last image that had come in from it was a fleeting glimpse of razor-like claws reaching for it. Dustin swallowed hard as another of the squad's cameras went out. The only left one. It belonged to a soldier named Iverson.

Iverson came stumbling out of the kaiju corpse's mouth onto the platform. Sergeant Bible nearly blew a hole in Iverson's chest, only managing to hold his fire at the last possible second as he must have realized Iverson wasn't one of the creatures.

"They're right behind me!" Iverson wailed and raced to join Sergeant Bible and the five men with him.

Iverson wasn't kidding. In the time it took him to move far enough across the platform to reach Sergeant Bible and his men, a dozen or more of creatures surged out of the kaiju corpse's mouth in his wake. None of the creatures were alike. Some of them were shaped like humans though covered with scales and had mouths of gleaming razor teeth. One had the upper body of a man but its lower half was that of snake. Another resembled a giant spider, its eight legs ending in spear-like tips that rang out against the metal surface of the platform as it skittered towards Sergeant Bible's men. Yet another of the creatures had the head of a shark and the tail of scorpion arcing upwards from its back. It moved on four legs, screeching like a demon straight out of hell as it came.

"Fire at will!" Sergeant Bible ordered as his heavy shotgun thundered. The lead creature stumbled from the impact of the blast. The shotgun was powerful enough of a weapon to get penetration. Its slug ripped into the creature's ribcage as an explosion of black blood exploded from the gaping wound.

The men with Sergeant Bible opened fire too. A cacophony of gunfire echoed in the Cavern. One creature took a burst of fire to its shoulder that nearly severed one of its arms from its body. Another had its guts ripped apart as one of Sergeant Bible's men emptied his rifle's magazine into it. Sergeant Bible and his men were keeping the creatures at bay for the moment, but more and more of the things were emerging from the mouth of the kaiju corpse. The area of the platform directly in front of the corpse's mouth was littered with the bodies of half a dozen dead creatures. They slowed those moving over and around them towards the soldiers but not enough. The creatures were blindingly fast. Despite the barrage of gunfire and their brethren being mowed down beside them, some of the things made it through to reach Sergeant Bible and his men.

One of the creatures leaped at the soldier to Bible's right. The man screamed, trying to bring his weapon around to get a shot at it. Instead, the man's rifle found itself in the path of the claws that were slashing towards him. The force of the blow broke the rifle apart in the soldier's hands. It saved his life. Staggering backwards, he went for his sidearm as Sergeant Bible whirled, firing his shotgun into the creature's face at point-blank range. The creature's head disintegrated atop its shoulders. Its body thudded to rest at Sergeant Bible's feet. Sergeant Bible pumped another round into the shotgun's chamber and turned back to face the mass of creatures still erupting from the kaiju corpse's mouth.

A soldier raked the creature with the lower body of a snake with a stream of automatic fire that blew chunks of black-smeared meat and muscle from its torso. The creature thrashed about in pain. Its tail whipped around at the soldier. It only dealt him a glancing blow, but it was enough to force him over the platform's railing to topple to the Cavern floor below. His body struck the metal floor there with a sickening crash. The soldier lay still with red bubbling over his lips as his he fought to breathe and his eyes rolled up to show only whites.

Sergeant Bible knew that he and his men were going to be overrun if they stayed where they were. He wanted to shout for his men to fall back, but there was nowhere to fall back to. In order to get off the platform, they either had to jump or climb the ladder leading down from it. The distance was too great to attempt the first without risk of being seriously hurt or flat-out killed, and the second left them entirely open to the creatures. Their only choice as Sergeant Bible saw things was to take as many of the monstrous things emerging from the mouth of the kaiju's corpse with them that they could. The soldiers below in the Cavern couldn't really offer support. The angle was all wrong. The platform itself blocked the bulk of their line of fire.

A creature on four legs that resembled a deformed ant came charging across the platform at Sergeant Bible. He racked a shell in his shotgun and lowered the weapon, adjusting his aim. The thing barely stood four feet tall at its shoulders. His shotgun bucked in his hands as he fired. The creature's first leg was literally melded into the front of its body. Sergeant Bible's shot reduced it to an inwardly curving depression of mangled tissue and shattered chitin. The creature stopped in its tracks by the blast, froze in its rush forward, then toppled to rest on its side, its legs flailing about in the air. Sergeant Bible figured the leg movement was just nerve impulses. He hoped he was right because he didn't have ammo to waste double tapping the thing. There was only two shells left in his shotgun and he needed to make them count.

"We have to get off this platform!" Iverson shouted at him.

The soldier who had lost his rifle had his handgun drawn. His 1911 thundered as he fired half its magazine into a creature that looked like a cross between a man and turtle. The soldier's bullets pinged and sparked away from the thing's shell with doing any real damage to it.

"Aim for its head!" Sergeant Bible yelled at the soldier.

The soldier moved to do just that but never got the chance. A snarling creature with a snout like a rat's and scales instead of fur bounded into him from his left side. The rat thing and the soldier disappeared over the edge of the platform together.

Iverson had given up trying to hold the creatures at bay and was already clinging to the top of the platform's ladder leading to the Cavern below. Iverson must have caught Sergeant Bible's glance at him because he shouted, "No choice, sir! We go down or we die!"

Sergeant Bible couldn't argue with the man as he realized with a start that the two of them were the only two left alive on the platform. "Get going then!" Sergeant Bible shouted back. "I'll hold them for you!"

Iverson hadn't stuck around to protest his sacrifice though. The man was already climbing downward as Sergeant Bible slid into position in front of the top of the ladder. In that moment, Sergeant Bible knew he was dead. He snatched a grenade from his belt and lobbed it at the mass of abominations that continued to pour out of the kaiju corpse's mouth. Even as he threw it, he was bringing his shotgun up into a ready position.

The explosion from the grenade shook the platform and sent bits and pieces of the monsters struck by its blast flying. The platform shuddered under his feet, but Sergeant Bible kept his balance. A creature flashing its razor-like teeth at him darted toward him. Bracing his shotgun against his shoulder, Sergeant Bible fired a blast directly into the thing's chest. It was one of the bipedal monsters, and it staggered backwards as the shot ripped apart the center of its ribcage. Sergeant Bible pumped his last round into his shotgun's chamber and finished the monster where it lay twitching in front of him. Black blood splattered upwards as his last shot blew a fist-sized hole in the thing's back as it flopped about.

Sergeant Bible looked up to see that another of the creature was already on him. Its scorpion-like tail shot upwards into his body through his guts, its end emerging from between his lips as the tail twisted about inside of him.

****

Iverson dropped the last few feet to the Cavern floor as he let go of the ladder. As his boots thudded onto the metal floor there, he saw that there were a great many of the monsters already down off the platform and engaging the soldiers in the Cavern. Iverson saw that two of the five soldiers acting as the backup squad were already dead. The other three were fighting for their lives. He knew Colonel Pitt had held a few men in reserve outside the Cavern. It was unlikely that the colonel was going to send them in at this point though. Their desperate defense of the Cavern was quickly becoming nothing more than a massacre.

The main door to the Cavern was already closed and locked into place. It made more sense for the colonel to write off the men inside and try to hold the creatures at the door if they were able to break through it. The doors were made of thick, reinforced steel so Iverson hoped that the creatures wouldn't be able to. If they got loose into Alpha Station, that was all she wrote for everyone in the base built around the Cavern.

There were several of the creatures crawling about on the Cavern's walls. Their ability to do so meant that even the main doors being locked down might not contain them. There was also the balcony on the upper-most level and the heating vents for the creatures to use to escape. The creatures didn't seem too intelligent but he wasn't going to put figuring out that those exit points existed beyond their range of feral, instinctual cunning.

"I'm out!" one of the soldiers cried.

"Here!" another shouted, tossing the first man a fresh magazine.

The first soldier caught the mag and rammed it home as a creature with the body and arms of a human-sized squid came stalking across the Cavern's floor at him. The thing moved on its two primary tentacles using them as legs as the creature's other tentacles slashed about madly around its body. The soldier held the trigger of his rifle tight, emptying the entirety of his new magazine into the beast. Its body was apparently as soft as that of the squid it resembled. It burst apart in a shower of shredded flesh and goo.

The metal floor of the Cavern smoked where the squid thing's blood landed.

"That thing's blood was freaking acid!" the soldier who had killed it yelled and they were his last words. Another creature, similar to the first one that had emerged from the kaiju's corpse, dropped on top of him from the ceiling above. The poor guy didn't even have time to scream as the first swipe of the thing's claws removed the top of his helmet and most of the upper part of his skull along with it. The second swipe of its claws claimed his eyes, his nose, and most of his top row of teeth, leaving rivers of flowing red in their wake.

Iverson and the remaining two soldiers were making their way towards the Cavern's doors. He didn't think for an instant that any of them truly believed those doors would open to allow them to escape. Iverson figured, just like him, that the other soldiers planned to simply have the doors at their backs so as to limit the angles the creatures could come at them.

Iverson and one of the soldiers reached the door, putting their backs against it, and keeping their eyes and blazing weapons forward. The other soldier never made it. One of the creatures like a giant centipede came skittering across the floor and up his back as he ran. The man cried out as the thing's legs sunk into and ripped out of his back in rapid succession as it climbed his body. He fell forward onto his face but the impact wasn't enough to shake the centipede thing loose. It brought the pincers protruding in front of his mouth together through the sides of his neck. The soldier's eyes bugged as blood gushed from his open mouth and his scream turned into a geyser of red vomit.

Bullets raked the centipede thing's shoulders and head as Iverson laid into it. His bullets also dug into the body of the dead soldier it was on top of, but Iverson didn't give a crap. The man was dead and from the looks of things, no one was going to be retrieving his body anyway. He was food for the creatures now once they had finished with the battle.

Iverson glanced at the last soldier next to him and saw his own fear and desperation reflected in the man's eyes. The brief glance back the soldier gave him cost him his life. In that instant, a creature sprung forward, taking his head in its hands to slam his skull into the metal doors behind him. The soldier's head exploded like a rotten melon from the force of the impact. His body slid down the length of the door to the floor as Iverson brought his rifle around to take a shot at the creature that had killed him. The three-round burst from Iverson's rifle ripped holes in the side of the creature's neck at near point-blank range. It howled and dashed away, clutching at the wounds leaking black blood.

Colonel Pitt's voice was raging over Iverson's comm, but he wasn't listening. There was nothing that Colonel Pitt could say that would help him now. He was alone with a vast room of hungry monsters intent on feasting upon his flesh.

Iverson's rifle clicked empty as he tried to take a shot at a human-like creature on two legs with blood-slicked claws as it closed on him. Shifting his rifle around in his grip, he swung it like a club at the monster. Its butt caught the underside of the creature's chin, snapping its snarling mouth closed and causing it to stumble backwards. Iverson allowed the rifle to slip from his grasp as he went for his sidearm. Two more of the creatures were already on him. One of them that was shaped like a beetle and much shorter than most of the others gnawed on his knee. He felt his knee give out as the bones there was crushed and red spurted from where the thing's teeth worked at him. The other one, more human in shape, managed to clasp a three-fingered hand around his throat as Iverson brought his pistol. He didn't waste any more bullets or effort trying to stop the inevitable. He pressed the pistol's barrel to his temple and squeezed its trigger. Brain matter and bone fragments followed the bullet out of the gaping exit wound it left in the other side of his head.

****

Nicholson and Hyatt waited outside the bulkhead doors that led into the Cavern. Despite those doors being sealed, they had heard the entire battle over their comms. Nicholson clutched a lit flamethrower. Its pilot flame blazed blue and he kept a finger on the weapon's trigger. Hyatt was packing a SAW. The big man claimed he was used to firing the heavy weapon from his hip and had served in a heavy weapons squad before his assignment to Alpha Station. Nicholson believed him. The way Hyatt carried the SAW spoke volumes about his competence with it.

The two of them had waited for the order to open the doors to the Cavern and go in guns blazing, but that order had never come. That meant the situation inside was likely even worse than it sounded and it sounded grimmer than Hell. Several of the men inside the Cavern had died with their comms activated, and they both could still hear the sounds of flesh being ripped and chewed on by hungry teeth. It was pretty dang clear that everyone who had been inside the Cavern was dead. *Fifteen men total and all gone in a matter of minutes*, Nicholson thought. That only left the two of them, Colonel Pitt, Kennedy, who was up top somewhere in Alpha Station, and the base's pilots in terms of military personnel, and the pilots didn't really count. Sure, they had some combat training but not enough to go head to head with the things inside the Cavern and have a prayer of surviving.

"They're all dead," Hyatt commented in a voice not much above a whisper.

"I know," Nicholson nodded as he answered.

"What in the devil do we do now?" Hyatt asked, staring at him.

Nicholson shrugged and shook his head. "I don't know. I just don't know. I guess we hold here and pray to God that those things don't make through those doors."

"Do you think they can?" Hyatt frowned.

"What the hell, man?" Nicholson snapped, his own nerves getting the better of him. "How would I know?"

Hyatt hefted the SAW he held. "If they do, we'll frag the bastards."

Nicholson didn't know for sure if Hyatt was just putting on a show for his sake or if the big man really was a dumb as he sometimes looked. Eying the corridor around them, Nicholson was already working out a path for them use in a fighting retreat if the monsters did make it through.

"Sure, man," Nicholson tried to sound braver and more professional than he was feeling at the moment. "We'll frag the bastards. As many as we can anyway."

"Think we should call the colonel?" Hyatt asked.

"We're going to hold our position until he contacts us with new orders. Got it?" Nicholson explained carefully. Technically, he was the senior officer, but if the big man broke rank and abandoned his post at the Cavern's doors, there wasn't a heck of lot Nicholson could do to stop him short of turning his flamethrower on the giant of man, and that wasn't something he was going to do.

After a moment passed of them staring at each other, Hyatt finally spoke again. "What if they do really get through, Nick?"

"Then God have mercy on us, buddy, because we're all dead men," Nicholson told him bluntly.

****

Colonel Pitt and Dustin had watched the horrors on the Cavern unfold as they had happened. Dustin wiped the dregs of his latest round of vomiting from his lips with the backside of his hand and rose up from the trashcan he was bent over at his seat in front of the Cavern's control console. Colonel Pitt was nearly foaming at the mouth behind him. It was as if the colonel was in shock. The man clearly hadn't expected fifteen heavily armed and highly trained men to be an insufficient force to stop the young kaiju from emerging from their mother's corpse.

Dustin ran his fingers through his sweat-slicked hair and stared at Colonel Pitt. "What do we do now, sir? The Cavern is as locked down as we can make it, but I don't think that's going to be enough to stop those monsters from getting out and into the base."

Colonel Pitt's angry gaze fell upon him. The man looked like he was about ready to hurl himself through the control room's window and into the Cavern to go after the creatures out there with his bare hands.

When the Cavern had been constructed, there had been two safety features built into it. One was a standard self-destruct. Charges were planted throughout its walls and ceiling in case the place needed to brought down fast. Dustin knew better than to think that the colonel was going to order its use. Colonel Pitt would lose too much for resorting to that, and the project's financial backers would have him up on charges as a scapegoat in a heartbeat if he did. The other safety feature was actually built into the fire suppression system. In addition to the normal chemical fire extinguishers in the Cavern's ceiling, there were nozzles designed to let loose liquid nitrogen on its interior. Those had been designed in case something went wrong with the kaiju corpse's slowed thawing and extraction process. They were designed to refreeze everything in the Cavern with the press of a button. That system had been nicknamed the Freezer by the work crews and techs like himself, though Dustin hadn't been the one to come up with it and thought it sounded sort of retarded.

"Activate the nitrogen throwers," Colonel Pitt ordered him.

Dustin nodded. "Yes, sir."

They both knew that there was no one left alive inside the Cavern to be threatened by the rain of liquid death they were about to hit it with. The only things still moving around in there were the young kaiju that had escaped from the giant corpse.

As Dustin reached from the button, one of the small kaiju slammed into the control room's window. It had the body of a man covered in scales. The force of its body striking the window sent spider-web cracks across the reinforced glass. Dustin instinctively drew back from the console as the thing had smashed into the window directly in front of it. Colonel Pitt had drawn the pistol holstered at his side and held its barrel aimed at the snarling abomination staring at them through the fractured window with burning, yellow eyes. For a fraction of a second, Dustin thought the colonel was going to open fire on it. The colonel must have realized at the last second too that doing so would only finish to shattering the already weakened window to allow the thing to come crashing into the control room with them.

"Mother pus bucket!" Colonel Putt yelled, lowering his weapon. "Hit that blasted button!"

Dustin forced himself to find the courage to lean forward again despite the snarling thing smearing blood that wasn't its own from its lips onto the glass in front of him. He stabbed the button and the Freezer activated as the creature on the window reared back one of its clawed hands and put it through the weakened glass.

The nitrogen sprayers hosed the interior of the Cavern with their contents. Creatures caught in their spray howled and shrieked as either parts of their bodies or their entire forms froze in an instant. Flesh cracked and broke apart as they continued to try to move. Dustin saw the ones trying to rip through the Cavern's massive, sealed doors die where they stood. Others though managed to escape the deluge of liquid death that poured down at them. He saw more than one tear off a cover to a heating vent and disappear into it. Then, Dustin didn't have time focus on anything but the monster that toppled through the control room's window in an explosion of flying glass shards that flew towards him.

Dustin screamed as a shard of glass slashed open his right shoulder as it passed him. Another embedded itself in his chest with a dull thump that sent pain flaring through him. He heard Colonel Pitt cursing at the top of his lungs as the military man fired his pistol in rapid succession at the small kaiju that leaped over his own hunching form at the colonel. His first shot hammered into the center of the kaiju's chest. Two more followed it. They got penetration and hurt the kaiju but didn't stop it. As it landed on the control room's floor and rose to its full five foot height, three more bullets slammed into it. One clipped its right shoulder, spinning it about. A fraction of a second later, the other two pierced its side. The kaiju was wailing like a banshee as it twisted around to slash at Colonel Pitt. Its claws made contact with his outstretched hand holding his pistol. The claws removed the hand holding the pistol at its wrist. Colonel Pitt grunted in pain and reeled backwards away from the kaiju as it pressed its advantage, lunging at him.

Not having a real weapon, Dustin used the only thing he had at hand. Ignoring the pain from the shards of glass, he heaved the trashcan of vomit from the floor next to his seat into the kaiju's face. The vomit splashed over the kaiju. The vomit's sickening smell filled the small room as the kaiju wiped at it eyes, trying to clear them. The desperate act bought Colonel Pitt some time. Dustin saw Colonel Pitt fling open the control room's door and throw himself through it. Cursing the colonel for a coward, Dustin gritted his teeth and shoved himself up from his seat at the control room's console. He was about to hurl himself across the room and towards the doorway when another kaiju plunged into the control room through the shattered window. The beast was partially frozen from the rain of liquid nitrogen that had rained over it when the Freezer had been activated. Its legs broke apart under the weight of its body as it landed on the control room's floor. Frozen chunks of kaiju meat and pieces of solid black blood bounced away from its upper body as it thudded onto the floor in Dustin's path. There was no time to even attempt to dodge the claws that lashed out him as the kaiju sought its vengeance. The fronts of Dustin's thighs were shredded by the thing's claws as cried out in fear and pain. He went rolling to the floor beyond where the dying kaiju thrashed about. He looked up to see its yellow eyes fixed on him as it dragged itself across the control room's floor with its claws towards him.

Dustin tried to kick at it, but ripples of pain shot through him from the attempt to move his badly wounded legs and he failed. The kaiju grabbed him by one of his ankles and yanked him to it. Dustin noticed the other kaiju had vanished through the doorway out into the corridor beyond in pursuit of Colonel Pitt. His mind barely had time to process that information before the kaiju that pulled him over to it sunk its glistening teeth into his throat. His scream became a strangled gargling noise as hot blood exploded from where the kaiju's teeth worked at his neck in a hurried frenzy to finish him before it died. And it did...

****

Ashley, Laura, and Dr. Pressley Looked up from their work as Alpha Station's alarm klaxons began to blare.

"What the...?" Dr. Pressley started getting up from where he was sitting.

Ashley frowned. "I'd say that means the colonel found more kaiju."

"And likely more than he could handle," Laura added.

"What do we do?" Dr. Pressley asked.

"We stay exactly where we are and wait to hear what's going on out there," Ashley said firmly in a tone that left no room for argument.

Through the lab's open door, something could be heard moving about in the corridor outside it. Whatever it was, Ashley could tell it was moving fast.

"Laura!" she ordered, "Get that door closed!"

"Yes, ma'am," Laura cried racing for the door. As she reached it, a blood-smeared face appeared in it. Laura screamed a high-pitched cry of pure terror that echoed off the walls of the lab.

Dr. Pressley, Ashley, and Laura found themselves staring at Colonel Pitt. The colonel shoved Laura from his path as he dove into the lab and slammed a fist against the door's control panel. The door slammed closed behind him as he looked frantically about the lab.

"What in the Hades is going on?" Ashley demanded, advancing on him. She suddenly realized just how pale his skin was. All of his exposed flesh was covered in sweat and his pupils were dilated. The man was in shock. Ashley felt her heart skip a beat behind her ribs as she noticed Colonel Pitt's right hand had been severed at its wrist.

"No time!" he spat at her. "It's...right behind me!"

Colonel Pitt stumbled forward, nearly collapsing onto her but caught himself at the last second. "Find a weapon," he stammered at her.

Something smashed into the door from its exterior side. Laura screamed again as something raked across the metal of the door like fingernails on a blackboard. The door shuddered in its frame but held.

"No time..." the colonel rasped again. "That door...won't keep it out."

Dr. Pressley looked ready to run for his life, but there was nowhere to run to. The door was the only way in or out of the lab. Laura had snatched up a scalpel from one of the lab's work table and clutched it like a knife.

Cradling the bleeding stub of his right arm to his chest, Colonel Pitt gestured at the lab's fire extinguisher with his other hand. Ashley ran to get it as the thing in the corridor struck the door again. This time, the door's metal dented inward from the force of its blow.

"I... I wouldn't even be alive," Colonel Pitt stuttered. "The only reason I am... that I ran into one of Rigger's workers. The kaiju got him instead of me."

"You're in shock," Laura told the colonel, practically shoving the man into a chair.

Ashley returned to stand beside Colonel Pitt where he now sat at her workstation with the fire extinguisher in hand. She popped its pin and shook it up as she looked the colonel over.

"I warned you to let me have a go at making sure the smaller kaiju inside the corpse stayed dormant when you sent your men in," Ashley grumbled.

She knew the colonel was hurting badly because he didn't argue with her.

"Do you know how many of the kaiju we're dealing with?" Ashley asked.

Colonel Pitt shook his head. "No idea. There were dozens that I saw come out of her, but Dustin and I managed to activate the Freezer protocol. It may have re-iced most of them. The one chasing me... It came through the control room's window right as the Freezer protocol activated. It wasn't hit by the sprayers."

"Do you think it's gone?" Dr. Pressley suddenly interrupted.

Ashley realized that after the second blow on the lab's door, the kaiju in the corridor had gone quiet.

"I doubt it," Ashley answered. "It's likely just looking for an easier way in."

"Or it could have spotted someone else out there and went after them," Laura said, sounding a touch too hopeful about it.

"How many men did you lose?" Ashley asked, placing a hand on Colonel Pitt's shoulder as she nodded at Laura, signaling for her to fetch the lab's first aid kit.

"Fifteen," Colonel Pitt admitted reluctantly. "At least fifteen."

"Sweet goodness," Dr. Pressley croaked. "Given how many that first creature took out, that's pretty much all of them, isn't it?"

Colonel Pitt nodded. "Nicholson and Hyatt are on watch outside the Cavern's main doors and Kennedy is up top. Other than them, only the pilots are left."

"Great," Laura said, sarcasm dripping from her. "So that only leaves us and whatever workers and support staff are left."

"Not helping," Ashley mouthed at Laura from where she had moved behind the colonel.

Laura unlocked and flipped open the first aid kit going to work on the colonel's stub of a wrist. "This is going to hurt like the devil kicking you in the balls," she warned him. "Can't be helped though."

Colonel Pitt grunted through gritted teeth, shifting around in his chair as she poured alcohol over what remained of the end of his arm and then went to work bandaging it up as tightly as she could.

"You've lost a lot of blood," Ashley said. "It's a miracle that you are even still conscious."

"Been...hurt bad...before," Colonel Pitt managed to answer her. "I'll live."

"Ashley." Dr. Pressley grabbed her by the arm, drenched in sweat born of fear and a mad look in his eyes. "What are we going to do?"

"Not much we can do right now, Pressley," she told him. "We can start by getting on the comm and seeing who else is out there though. If we're lucky, there might be someone still alive and in a position to help us."

"Sounds like a plan," Laura agreed. "I'm on it!"

****

Dr. Gallenger didn't know what to make of the sudden blaring of Alpha Station's alarm klaxons. He knew that the colonel's men were supposed to be heading into the kaiju corpse to see if it held any more lethal and hungry surprises. The alarm had to mean something had gone wrong, but he didn't know if he should be preparing to receive more wounded or trying to get the hell out of dodge. He had just agreed to let Sam go when the alarms began. Dr. Jessi now stood watching him.

"Everything okay, Doc?" Sam asked.

"From the sound of things," he answered, "no, not at all."

Sam nodded. "Figured as much. I may be new here, but I know I trouble when I hear it. Is there any protocol for something like this?"

"Dr. Jessi…" Dr. Gallenger started.

"I told you to call me Sam," Dr. Jessi stopped him.

"Sam," Dr. Gallenger began again. "No, there really isn't. In all the time this base has been up and running, we've never had anything like that smaller kaiju getting loose before happen. I'd say these klaxons we're hearing mean there are a lot more of them loose now."

"That's a pretty big jump to make there, isn't it, Doc?" Sam pointed out. "The colonel would have been prepared to hold them in the Cavern if more of the things got out. He doesn't strike me as the type to take a chance on more of those things getting loose even if he wasn't expecting whatever his men ran into when they went into the corpse."

"I've found it's best to be prepared for the worst," Dr. Gallenger said, shooting him a smirk tinged with sarcasm.

"Hey, what was that?" Sam asked as something thudded about in the heat vent across the room from where they stood.

Dr. Gallenger stared at the cover of the heating vent like a man who had just seen his own death coming.

Three razor-like claws emerged through the vent's cover. They glistened redly in the light of the room as something inside the vent snarled loudly.

"Run!" Dr. Gallenger shouted as the thing inside the vent shoved off its cover and emerged from the vent to drop onto the floor. The small kaiju only stood slightly over four feet tall. Its body was covered in reptilian scales from head to toe. The creature was roughly human in shape though its arms were longer than those of a man's, resembling those of a primate. Each arm ended in a three-fingered hand of razor sharp claws. The kaiju's eyes glowed yellow with rage and hunger even in the room's light, like miniature suns burning in their sockets. The creature's lips stretched thin as they were pulled back into a fresh snarl that showed the rows of sharply pointed teeth within its mouth.

Sam was already running towards the door that led out into the corridors of Alpha Station when Dr. Gallenger started after him only to suddenly stop.

"The chief!" Dr. Gallenger yelled. "We can't just leave him!"

Sam spun about, his eyes already scanning the room for something to use as a weapon. He spotted a walking cane propped up against the wall near the doorway and snatched it up. Sam suffered no delusion that the weapon would do much against the snarling kaiju, but it was better than being completely empty-handed.

The kaiju sprang at Dr. Gallenger as he altered his path and raced towards the room containing the chief. He shoved a rolling chair at the monster in the hope of slowing it down. The move caught the kaiju off guard. It collided with the chair, getting tripped up, and careened into the room's wall with a loud thud. The thing recovered instantly and started for Dr. Gallenger again with nothing to block its path this time.

Sam watched as the kaiju hurled itself through the air in a cat-like leap which carried it onto Dr. Gallenger. It landed on the doctor, its claws sinking into the meat of his shoulders to hold itself there.

Dr. Gallenger was screaming as he toppled backwards to the floor with the kaiju clinging to him. The thing jerked its claws free of Dr. Gallenger's shoulders and started batting his face back and forth from one clawed hand to the other. Each hit was also a slash that mangled Dr. Gallenger's cheeks, sending blood splattering all over the floor around where the two of them fought. Dr. Gallenger's body went limp after about the third such hit, though the kaiju continued to tear at the man's face, shredding it beyond recognition.

Sam looked over at the doorway leading into Chief Rigger's room in utter shock as the chief came lumbering through it with a chair in his hands. The chief was a big man. He hefted the chair above his head and brought it down onto the kaiju's back with such force that it shattered there. The impact slammed the kaiju to the floor and sent it rolling away from Dr. Gallenger's corpse.

"Get out of here, Dr. Jessi!" Chief Rigger roared snatching up a laptop from a nearby work desk. "Someone has to warn whoever is left out there!"

Sam started to protest. He didn't want to leave the chief to die at the kaiju's claws. He knew the chief was right though. If he stayed, he'd only die too. Not knowing what to say, Sam spun about towards the door and darted through it.

"Come on, you bastard!" he heard Chief Rigger yelling behind him as he sprinted along the corridor away from Alpha Station's medical section. A loud smashing noise followed the chief's shout. He almost slowed his frantic pace in the hopes that the chief had somehow defeated the kaiju, but then he heard the chief screaming. Sam's legs pumped beneath him as he poured on all the speed his body could muster and ran like hell onward through Alpha Station's corridors.

****

Caroline had been on her way topside when the alarms began to blare. She and other two pilots, Fred and Charles, were headed up to run some system checks on the base's helicopters and make sure they were fueled up and ready to go. Colonel Pitt had ordered them to do it, though none of them fully understood the urgency with which he had given the order. They had been laughing and cutting up one minute, making jokes about Dr. Pressley's love life, and the next, they had found themselves fighting for their lives.

A creature that could only be a kaiju like the one that had gotten into Alpha Station earlier came tearing around a bend in the corridor at them. It moved like lightning with scales. Charles was dead before they even knew what was happening. The thing gutted him with the razor sharp claws of its hands spilling the purple strands of his intestines all over the corridor floor at his feet. Charles' eyes had bugged with shock and pain in the fraction of a second before a second swipe of the thing's claws removed his head from his shoulders. As Charles' head bounced along the floor of the corridor, Fred went for the gun holstered on his hip. All of the pilots were allowed to carry sidearms when on duty, but only Fred made a point of always being armed. He was the paranoid type, and this time, it had paid off. The small kaiju leaped at Fred as his pistol cleared its holster and came up firing. Fred managed to put two rounds into the kaiju's upper body before it slammed into him. Caroline wasn't the screaming sort. Instead, she flew into action as well, racing towards the closest comm panel on the corridor's wall. She stabbed it on.

"We've got one of those monsters loose on level one!" she yelled into the comm panel. "We need backup. Now!"

The only answer she got was the crackle of static. Something was wrong with Alpha Station's internal comms. She slammed an angry fist into the panel and whirled about to check on Fred. The kaiju had Fred pinned to the floor. Blood flowed from where the thing's claws had already dug deep gashes into his shoulders and chest during their scuffle. Fred's pistol fired again, but the shot went wild as he wasn't able to fully bring the pistol to bear on the thing that was on top of him. The bullet sparked off the metal wall of the corridor.

Caroline looked around desperately for something, anything she could use to come to Fred's aid. There wasn't anything to be found though. All she could do was watch as her friend struggled against the monster that wanted to rip open his flesh and cover itself in his blood.

Working up her courage, Caroline sprinted to where the two of them wrestled. Hauling off, she lashed out with her right boot, kicking the kaiju dead on, the tip of her boot hitting against the underside of its chin. The kaiju's head snapped back as its mouth was knocked closed. The blow gave Fred the time to seize a momentary advantage over it. He pressed the barrel of his Glock 43 to the side of the kaiju's skull and squeezed the weapon's trigger. The point-blank shot blew chunks of skull bone and meat from the opposite side of the creature's head where the bullet tore through it, leaving a gaping exit wound in its wake. The kaiju's body slumped onto Fred. He caught its weight with a loud grunt and strained to roll its body away from him onto the corridor floor next to where he lay.

Caroline gasped as the kaiju corpse rolled off Fred and saw just how badly it hurt him before he had managed to end it. She hadn't seen it happen, but the kaiju sunk a set of its claws up and under his ribcage. The open wound stretched a solid foot long across Fred's chest. Blood bubbled out of it with each wheezing breath that Fred fought to take.

She knelt next to Fred, taking one of his hands in hers. "Hang in there. Help is on the way."

Fred shook his head, red pooling inside his mouth to coat his teeth and leak from the corners of his lips. "Done...for," he croaked at her. "You need to..."

And then, just like that, Fred was gone and Caroline found herself alone in a corridor full of corpses. She sat there staring at Fred from what seemed like a long time.

Tears formed in her eyes, but she refused to let them flow, instead turning them into anger. If there were more of those monsters out there, they were going to pay.

Caroline slowly rose to her feet. She got her bearings as to where she was in Alpha Station. When she started moving again, it wasn't towards the lift that would have taken her topside; it was in the direction of the base's armory. All of the officer-level military personnel had a key to it, and as one of the base's pilots, so did she.

****

Downey, Bryan, and Jacobs had drawn the short straws and gotten stuck with cleaning up the mess hall from the earlier creature attack. They had been hard at it for hours now. Downey paused in his mopping up of dried blood to wipe at the sweat on his brow.

"Change that music!" he shouted at Jacobs. The woman was obsessed with eighties songs, and if he had to listen to one more Duran Duran track, he swore he was going to choke the life out of her with his bare hands.

Hungry Like the Wolf had just begun to thunder through the mess' speaker system as Jacobs yelled back at him. "No way," she said. "I am not putting on any of that crap you listen to."

"Metal," Downey muttered, more to himself than her. "It's called metal."

He shot a look in Bryan's direction. "Back me up here, buddy. I can't take this crap anymore."

Bryan laughed. "I'd like something a bit more classical myself. How about some Billy Joel?"

"Arrggh!" Downey scrunched up his face. "You people really have no musical taste whatsoever."

"Fine." Jacobs sneered at him and turned off the music. As she did, the three of them looked up at the mess hall's ceiling, realizing that the base's alarm klaxons were howling for the first time.

"Holy…" Bryan blurted out.

"You don't think…" Jacobs started.

"Couldn't be," Downey said, shaking his head. "That *thing* was one of a kind. There couldn't be more of them."

"I wish the chief were here," Jacobs commented, looking scared out her mind.

"Now look," Downey told her and Bryan. "There is absolutely no reason to panic. We don't have a clue what's actually happening yet."

"Yeah," Bryan agreed, "and that is the scary part."

The three of them looked up at the mess hall's broken ceiling again where it had caved in when the creature that had caused all the damage had attacked.

"I don't know about you two, but I'm done," Bryan said. "I'm headed to my quarters, and I ain't coming out until those klaxons are shut down and someone has made a base wide call that everything's okay."

"That's strange," Jacobs commented, apparently thinking over what Bryan had just said. "It's just the alarm. There's no one telling us what's happening or what to do. They normally do that, don't they?"

"Not always." Downey shrugged, trying to blow off her concern as things were bad enough already. "Like I said, there is no reason for us to panic yet."

"Says you," Jacobs snapped at him, the tension in the mess getting the best of her.

"Hey!" Bryan yelled. "What was that?"

"What was what?" Downey asked.

"Didn't you hear that?" Bryan asked, frowning. "It sounded like gunfire from somewhere out there in the corridors."

"You're just playing around now," Downey warned him. "We don't have time for crap like that. We need to get busy finding out what's actually going on."

"And how do we do that?" Jacobs asked, standing near the comm unit on the mess hall's wall. "I already tried the comm while you two were arguing. It's not working. All I am getting on it is static."

"I am thinking some serious doo-doo has gone down out there and we've been left to fend for ourselves," Bryan said. "You guys do what you want. You know where I am headed."

Bryan was moving towards the mess hall's exit when the creature came bursting into the wide, table-filled room. The creature resembled some sort of reptilian cross between a dog and a cat. It moved on four legs with an almost unbelievable speed. The thing plowed into Bryan before he even had time to scream, taking him to the floor. Its razor teeth sunk into his body time and time again as it ravaged him, shaking his body back and forth as it ripped away the flesh from his bones.

Downey heard Jacobs scream and saw her dash off for the kitchen area at the mess hall's rear. Keeping a tight hold on his mop, as it was the only thing close a weapon that he had, Downey ducked beneath the closest table and prayed that the creature wouldn't notice him. Right now, it was pretty focused on eating on Bryan, though he knew that wouldn't last forever.

The creature wolfed down mouthfuls of Bryan's guts and other chunks of his body for some time, smacking its lips with each bite. It had to know that both he and Jacobs were in the mess with it, but it didn't seem to care and certainly didn't think of them as a threat. When the thing had its fill of Bryan, it looked up in the direction of the kitchen that Jacobs had fled into. The demon hound's thickly muscled four legs carried across the mess as it bounded for the kitchen. Jacobs must have seen it coming because she started screaming again. A knife came flying through the doorway of the kitchen. It spun end over end through the air at the demon hound but missed the creature entirely to clatter to the floor far behind it.

As the creature reached the doorway of the kitchen, Jacobs was suddenly there to meet it. She swung a frying pan at the thing's head. The metal of the pan smashed into its skull with the sound of cracking bone. The demon hound staggered, stunned by the unexpected blow as Jacobs rushed it, swinging the pan again. She brought the pan down again onto the top of its skull with the loud ring of metal smashing against armor-like scales and bone. This time, the demon hound was ready for her. It shrugged off her second blow and took a swipe at her. Jacobs cried out as its claws tore her right leg from her body at the knee. Blood spurting from the stump of where her lower leg had been, Jacobs crashed to the floor in front of the demon hound. Despite the pain she had to be in, she still had some fight though. She viciously swung the pan at the creature, managing to connect with the side of its jaw as it lunged at her. The impact batted the creature's head to the side, preventing its teeth from shredding her throat. The demon hound shook itself as if clearing its head before it moved again. As Jacobs brought the pan around at it again in another swing, its snout-like face shot forward to catch her arm in its teeth. They bit through her arm, crunching bone, and snapped it in two. Jacobs wailed like dying cat as she drew what was left of her arm back and up so she could look at it with wide, disbelieving eyes.

The demon hound gave a snort as it crawled onto her body, pinning her shoulders to the mess hall's floor with its forward feet. A long, forked tongue rolled out of its open mouth to lick at the blood which had splattered onto Jacob's face. She was screaming and thrashing about beneath the monster, trying to break free of it.

Downey wasn't a hero. He had never been one or even though of himself in such a way. Something within him snapped though as he watched the horrid scene unfolding before him. He knew he was the only hope that Jacobs had. Leaping to his feet, mop in hand, a wild battle cry escaped his lips as he charged across the mess towards the demon hound. He swung his mop like a baseball bat, shattering it over the demon hound's back. The creature barely flinched in response to the blow. Its yellow eyes turned to look up at him as he took the shattered remains of the mop and rammed it downwards like a spear at the creature, his entire weight behind the movement. The pointed end of the broken mop barely pierced the monster's scales before it snapped again, and Downey found himself falling onto the monster. He landed on it hard, forcing both his weight and its own down onto Jacobs. Downey heard her breath leave her lungs in a pained grunt. Her body seemed to sink inward beneath the two of them as her ribs gave way to their combined weight. Jacobs' eyes rolled up in her sockets as they fluttered closed and red began to seep from the corners of her mouth.

The demon hound rose up, throwing him from its back. Downey bounced several feet across the floor before a table very painful stopped him. The world spun and his vision clouded for a fraction of a second before he was able to collect himself. By the time he had, it was too late. The demon hound was on him.

Downey's hand caught a hold of the demon hound's shoulders, trying to keep its teeth at bay, but the monster was far too strong for him. It effortlessly pushed its snout closer to him, even as he shoved with all his might against its shoulders. Downey did the only thing he could think of. He rammed his head forward, smashing it into the creature's face. The demon hound's teeth cut his forehead as he made contact, but his desperate act saved his life. The startled demon hound reared back, shaking its head, allowing him to roll away from it.

Leaping to his feet, Downey sprinted for the mess hall's exit. He heard the demon hound growl behind him and then its footfalls as it started after him. The next thing he knew, he was laying on the floor with the monster on his back. Pain seared through him as its claws dug into him. The last thing Downey saw was a piece of bone that might have been a part of his spinal column go flying over his head to clatter onto the floor in front of him before everything went black and he didn't feel pain any longer.

****

Caroline crept through the corridors of Alpha Station. The armory was just up ahead of her now, and so far, she hadn't encountered any more of the creatures like that one that had torn apart the base's other two pilots before her eyes. She had passed several other bodies though along the way. Their blood had smeared the walls of the corridors and stained its floor. All of them had been workers from Chief Rigger's crew. The worst had been a woman that one of the creatures had crucified with her own bones. The monster had broken her legs and used pieces of their bones to nail her to the wall by her hands before driving a final piece of bone through her mouth. The sight of her naked and ravaged form had forced Caroline to stop and be sick before she could continue on. Caroline still refused to shed a single tear for any of the creatures' victims. She turned all of her fear and emotional pain into a sheer, burning desire for vengeance. That was why she was headed to the armory instead of topside where relative safety and the base's helicopters waited.

Rounding the bend in the corridor, Caroline spotted the door to the armory. The area appeared to be clear of any of the creatures that were lurking through Alpha Station in search of prey. She checked in one direction then the other to be as sure as possible before approaching the armory. Once there, she dug through her pockets and found the key card which would give her access to the armory and its contents. She slid the card through the lock's reader and the door swished open before her.

Caroline hadn't been to the armory since her initial tour of the base when she first arrived months ago. It was filled wall to wall with crates of ammo, grenades, and even one longer box that read "RPG" on its side. Hanging on the walls surrounding those crates were dozens upon dozens of rifles, machine guns, and pistols. There was also a rack of shotguns positioned near the rear of the room.

Making her choices carefully, she loaded up with as much as she could carry and still be able to move with any sort of reasonable speed. She strapped on a belt to which she fastened three holsters. They contained two Glock 43 pistols and a .44 Magnum revolver. She selected a P-90 and slung it onto her back by its carrying sling adding an AK-47 next to it. For her primary weapon, she picked an AA-12 automatic shotgun with a twenty-round drum magazine. She had heard the AA-12 offered both more accuracy and less recoil than the Saiga version. Caroline was tough and knew enough about firearms to be comfortable with them, but she also knew that recoil on something like an automatic shotgun could be a big issue for her and that was her main reason for opting for the AA-12.

As an afterthought, she collected several fragmentation grenades and added them to the sides of her backpack. A little extra, wide-spread firepower never hurt. Grenades weren't an ideal weapon to use in a place Alpha Station, as one detonating in the wrong spot could do damage to the structural integrity of the base's corridors, but their usefulness if she ran into more than she could handle with her weapons in terms of the creatures, it was better to have them than not.

The last thing Caroline donned before leaving the armory was a combat helmet. It contained a com-link tied to the soldiers of Colonel Pitt's unit. Finding anyone else still alive in Alpha Station was just as important as the gearing up she had just done. Caroline knew she couldn't fight the monsters loose in the base alone. Heck, she didn't even know how many of the monsters had come out of the giant corpse in the Cavern this time. Based on the bodies she had passed in the corridors though, she figured it was a great deal more than one this time.

Caroline activated the helmet's comm. "This is Lieutenant Caroline Edwards. Anyone who can hear me, please respond."

All she heard over the comm was the crackle of static, just like with the base's built-in comm system. She waited for a few seconds to tick by and then tried again.

"I say again, this is Lieutenant Caroline Edwards. Anyone still alive out there, please respond if you are able to do so."

"This is Hyatt," a deep, male voice answered her. "We read you, LT."

Caroline smiled at the sound of Hyatt's voice. "Thank God," she muttered. "Who's we, Hyatt?"

"This is Nicholson," another voice came over her helmet's comm. "Hyatt and I are on watch outside of the Cavern's entrance. The door is sealed and locked down tight."

"Copy that, Nicholson," Caroline replied. "What do you guys know about what's happening in Alpha Station?"

"Not much," Nicholson responded. "Colonel Pitt sent a group into the kaiju corpse. Whatever they found in there got out and massacred not only them, but we suspect everyone in the Cavern as well. We haven't even been able to raise the colonel and that tech Dustin who was on duty in the Cavern's control room since the crap hit the fan. We have been awaiting further orders since then."

"That door you're watching may be locked down, Nicolson, but it didn't stop the baby kaiju or whatever in Hades you want to call them from getting loose. They're inside Alpha Station and free to move about at will," Caroline told him. "I watched them kill Fred and Charles right in front of me. It was only the grace of God that the thing that got them didn't get me too."

"You can't be serious… That's insane," Nicholson protested. "Nothing has gotten out. We've been here the whole time."

"Think about it, Nicholson," Caroline explained. "There are more ways in and out of there than just that door."

After a brief pause, Nicholson called back, "Roger that, LT. So there's no reason for us to stay here then?"

"None whatsoever," Caroline agreed. "I am currently leaving the armory. Get your butts up here ASAP. I could use some backup. But be careful about it. Those creatures could be anywhere by now and only God knows how many of them there are."

"We copy, LT," Hyatt assured her. "We're on our way up."

Caroline ended the transmission, looking around the intersection of corridors was standing in to make sure none of the creatures had crept up on her while her attention had been occupied by Nicholson and Hyatt. The area appeared to still be free of the creatures. She desperately wanted to get moving, but she knew that waiting on the two soldiers to join her at her current location was the smartest thing she could do. Keeping her AA-12 at the ready, she settled in for what she hoped would only be a short wait.

****

Agent Markson stood over the small kaiju's still-twitching corpse, smoke trailing upwards from the barrel of his pistol towards the room's ceiling. The three holes his Desert Eagle had put in its skull had done the job of stopping it cold when it had ripped through the doorway of his quarters. Sometimes sleeping with your gun paid off. He had been recovering from his encounter with the first creature that had gotten loose in Alpha Station and taking some time to himself while Colonel Pitt oversaw the military expedition into the kaiju corpse. Cleary, things had gone very, very badly for the colonel and his men.

After checking to make sure there wasn't another of the creatures lurking in the corridor outside his room, Agent Markson turned moved to his desk to try the base's comm. It was dead. His cell was too. He had forgotten to put it on to charge when he crashed. Thankfully, he had been so strung out that he had slept in his clothes. All he needed was to grab a few extra magazines for his pistol and he was ready to move. Not that he had any idea of where to head to. If the kaiju he had just killed had been moving around Alpha Station freely enough to randomly find his room, there was no telling how many more of the things were out there or how much damage they had already done. Heading for the Cavern seemed a very bad idea. It was the source of the creatures, and if they had gotten out, that meant the colonel and likely most of his men were dead.

No, what he needed to do was get to somewhere with a working comm. The best bet for that was the surface. It seemed unlikely that the kaiju would head there as long as there was anyone alive in Alpha Station for them to hunt down. And he bloody well hoped that he wasn't the only survivor of whatever had happened. If he was, then that meant he would be the only target for however many of the kaiju were loose. It was a cold hope in that if there were others left alive he was using as decoys to cover his own escape, but if that's what it took then, that was what it took. He had to get in touch with the powers that be back home and let know them know just screwed the personnel of Alpha Station and the project were. Maybe he would even get lucky enough to find one of the base's three pilots topside and already waiting there. He recalled hearing Colonel Pitt order them to ready the helicopters and stay on standby while the expedition into the kaiju corpse took place.

Agent Markson stuffed the pockets of his jacket and pants with extra mags for his pistol and gave the base's comm one final try before truly deciding it was dead. He kept his Desert Eagle ready as he left his quarters behind and walked out into the corridor.

"Agent Markson!" someone yelled at him as they came running like a bat out of Hell around the bend in the corridor to his right. It took all his training not to put a bullet into the fool flying towards him. He had brought his pistol up, finger on the trigger, and barely stopped from squeezing it at the last second.

"Sam!" Agent Markson shushed Dr. Jessi. "Keep your bloody voice down!"

Sam skidded to a stop in front of him and reached out to grab him. "The kaiju! They're loose from the corpse. One of them just tore Dr. Gallenger and Chief Rigger apart in the medical section."

Agent Markson hauled back and slapped Sam hard across the face with the butt of his Desert Eagle to calm him down.

"Mother..." Sam cursed jerking a hand up to cover his aching cheek. "What did you do that for?"

"You needed it, man," Agent Markson growled. "Now keep your voice down before I have to do it again. Those things could be anywhere and any of them that are close by are going to hear you and come running."

Sam's face flashed in a startled expression as Agent Markson's words sunk in. He forced himself to a grip on his emotions. "Right," Sam nearly whispered, lowering his voice. "Sorry about that. It's just that—"

"The kaiju are loose in the base," Agent Markson finished for him. "I get it."

"I passed a bunch of bodies in the corridors on my way here. I couldn't even count them all," Sam stammered. "I knew I had to find you though. I figured if anyone was still alive and had a plan on what to do now, it was you."

Agent Markson laughed. "You give me too much credit, Sam. One of those things almost had me just a couple of minutes ago. It came bursting right into my quarters. I don't know if it smelled me in there or what. I didn't even know anything had gone wrong with the colonel's plan until it happened."

Sam stared at him. "But you do have a plan right?"

"Oh, I have a plan alright," Agent Markson said, flashing his teeth in a snarl-like grin. "It's called get the hell out of here."

"But the kaiju... Don't we need to stop them?" Sam protested.

"I don't know about you, Sam, but I'm not a superhero with kaiju claw-proof skin and super strength. I'm just a guy with a gun, some training, and a burning desire to live to see the sun rise tomorrow," Agent Markson said.

"We can't just..." Sam started again, but Agent Markson stopped him.

"We can and we will, Sam. It's not our job to save everyone else here or stop the monsters," Agent Markson argued. "It's up to us to make it out alive and let folks know what happened here so that someone else can back here and blow this place into a smoking crater so that these creatures don't get out into the world."

Agent Markson started walking and then paused to glance at Sam over his shoulder. "You with me or not?"

"I don't think I have a choice," Sam replied, shrugging.

"Right then," Agent Markson said with a smile. "Let's get moving. The sooner we make it topside, the better."

****

Nicholson and Hyatt finally arrived outside the base's armory where Caroline was waiting on them. She smiled as she saw the two of them emerge from the corridor to her left into the intersection she stood in.

"You guys sure took your time," she taunted them.

"Had a bit of trouble along the way." Nicholson returned her smile, holding up the severed head of a kaiju for her to see. "That sucker was as nasty as it looks like it was."

The head he held was human shaped but covered in layered brown scales. Its yellow eyes were glazed over and vacant, but even death, they sent a chill running along

Caroline's spine. Its mouth hung open, jaw distended, to show three rows of gleaming razor teeth.

Caroline noticed that Hyatt's shoulder was covered in a bandage with red still seeping through it.

"Thing took a bite out of me before I got it," Hyatt told her in a gruff tone.

"So, LT," Nicholson said, "we're here. You got a plan on what to do next?"

"Not really," Caroline answered honestly. She had been thinking things over the whole time she had been waiting on them and still hadn't come up with anything that didn't seem like more than desperate grasping at straws.

"I got one," Hyatt bellowed. "Let's call it fragging day and get the Hell out of this place. I mean, you're a pilot, aren't you, and there are three copters waiting right up there on the surface, right?"

Caroline thought about arguing with the big man but didn't see the point. She hadn't been able to get anyone else over the comm. It was very possible that the three of them were the only ones still alive in Alpha Station. Wandering around searching for others only put them further at risk with no certainty that they would find anything but more corpses like the ones she had seen earlier.

"I'd feel better if you were carrying something other than that," Caroline said, gesturing at Nicholson's flamethrower.

"I wouldn't," Nicholson said. "I've gotten attached to it. The kaiju we killed wasn't the only one that came at us on our way here. This thing scared the others away pretty good."

"Fine, keep it," Caroline relented. "Just be dang careful where you aim that thing."

"Yes, ma'am," Nicholson said with a nod.

"Anyone know if the lifts are still operating?" Caroline asked.

"None of the ones we tried were," Hyatt answered. "We had to take the stairs up from level three to get here."

The two soldiers had come up from the base's lowest level to the armory one level above it. The only other level of the base proper was its first, level one, and that was where they needed to go.

"Guess we're taking the stairs up then," Caroline said, sighing. "Best get to it then. The longer we stand around out here in this intersection, the more chance one of those things is going to stumble onto us."

"No argument from me, LT," Hyatt replied.

"You sure you're okay to handle that SAW you're carrying with your shoulder—" Caroline started.

"You let me worry about that," Hyatt said, sneering at her. "You just worry about getting us all out of here still kicking, LT."

"Okay." Caroline doubled checked her AA-12 to make sure it was ready for action and then said. "Nicholson, you got point. Lead us out of here."

****

The trio reached the stairwell leading up from level two to level one. Its lights were flickering and glowed dimly as if there was a disruption to their power. The dim light cast long shadows in the stairwell. The place would have been creepy to Caroline even if there hadn't been the chance that nightmarish monsters that had no right to exist in the real world might be waiting on them as they headed up the stairs.

Nicholson stayed on point as they moved as quietly as they could, considering the amount of weapons and ammo they were carrying. There were only three flights of wrap around stairs between where they entered the stairwell and the entrance to the base's first level above them, and they were clear of the kaiju. Caroline was beginning to feel like they had it made when the doorway to the first level above them exploded into the stairwell, flying over the rails of the stairs to plummet downwards into the darkness the base's deeper level three far below. The creature that came through it was a towering eight feet in height. It had three arms, two of them positioned like a human's, with the third growing out of the center of its chest. Two mouths flashed razor teeth beneath its yellow, bulbous eyes. It screeched as it saw them on the stairs below it.

"Light it up!" Caroline shouted a Nicholson.

The barrel of his flamethrower erupted, hosing the monster with a geyser of flame. The monster's screech rose in pitch as the flames washed over its scale-covered body. Nicholson continued to pour on the flames as the creature staggered about. Its blind stumbling carried it over the railing of the platform it was on. A loud thud echoed up through the stairwell as its body slammed into its bottom.

"Keep moving!" Hyatt yelled from behind Nicholson and Caroline.

The three of them rushed up the last of the stairs and through the broken doorway into the corridors of Alpha

Station's upper level. They fanned out around the doorway, prepared to engage anything else that came at them. The corridor was empty though.

Not far ahead of their position, the corridor branched off, one section leading to the right and another left.

"Head to the right!" Caroline ordered, shoving Nicholson back into motion.

Nicholson paused as he found his path partially blocked by the corpse of one of Chief Rigger's workers. The woman's body, or what was left of it anyway, lay in the center of the corridor in a pool of drying blood. Entire sections of her flesh had been gnawed from her bones. The distraction of the gory mess in front of him kept Nicholson from noticing the monster that hung upside down from the corridor's ceiling until it was too late. Nicholson screamed as the monster swung to fling itself onto him. One of its clawed hands batted the flamethrower from his hands and its other lashed out to plunge into his forehead.

Caroline flinched and tried to turn her face away as Nicholson's blood and brain matter exploded over her. The creature that had taken his life landed gracefully on the corridor's floor as Nicholson's lifeless form crumpled over. Caroline's AA-12 swung up as she squeezed the automatic shotgun's trigger. It thundered in the enclosed space of the corridor's walls. The monster was hurled backwards as the blast from her AA-12 sent it sprawling with its guts hanging out of the newly blown hole in its abdomen. Caroline removed her finger from the weapon's trigger, conserving ammo.

The creature was trying to drag itself away from her and the wicked weapon that had gutted it trailing long, black-slicked strands of its intestines behind it. Caroline took careful aim before she fired again. When she did, the carefully placed three-round burst she fired popped the monster's head like a ruptured pimple. The monster's black blood splashed onto the corridor walls.

"Nicholson!" Hyatt shouted, racing by her to his where his friend lay. The big man sunk to his knees next to Nicholson and looked on the verge of tears. Caroline grabbed him by one of his arms, trying to yank him to his feet, but she lacked the strength to do so.

"Come on, Hyatt!" she urged. "He's dead. There's nothing we can do from him now."

The big, hardened veteran looked up at her with sorrowful eyes and said, "We're all dead, aren't we? The two of us just haven't figured out it yet."

Caroline resisted the urge to bash him in the nose with the butt of her AA-12. Instead, she tried her best officer voice, "Get up, Hyatt! We have to keep moving!"

The big man slowly rose to his feet. "I don't think so, ma'am. I think I am going to stay right here and take as many of those fraggers with me as I can when they come."

From the look of anger and determination in Hyatt's eyes, Caroline knew that arguing with him would be pointless.

"I'll send help then," she told him and started running onward along the corridor.

"You do that," Caroline heard Hyatt laughing behind her.

****

All of Laura's attempt to raise someone, anyone, over Alpha Station's comm had failed. Colonel Pitt had fallen unconscious in the chair they had helped him into. Dr. Pressley appeared on the brink of a complete nervous breakdown. Ashley knew she had to do something. Staying in the lab was no longer an option. Though there had been no sign of whatever monster had attacked the lab's door from its exterior side, she knew their luck couldn't and wouldn't last. There were more means of getting into the lab at them than just its main door. She needed to find a way to get everyone working together as a coherent unit and on the move. Colonel Pitt's brief attempt at an explanation of what had happened in the Cavern when his men went into the kaiju corpse was enough to convince her that despite his attempts to stop the creatures, more than one of them had gotten out and was now wandering about Alpha Station in search of prey. The project was done for. All that mattered now was getting to somewhere safe where the creatures couldn't reach them. That meant they were going to have to venture out into the base and head for its topside buildings. Up there, they might stand a real chance of escaping this place before they got eaten.

Hefting the fire extinguisher from the lab, she tiptoed over to the door leading out into the corridor. Pressing her ear against it, she listened for any sign that the monster might still be out there waiting on its other side.

"What are you doing?" Dr. Pressley asked in a voice that was little more than a fear-filled whisper.

"We can't stay here," Ashley told him. "Laura's not been able to get a hold of anyone and even the alarm klaxons have gone silent."

"You can't be serious," Laura joined in the conversation, walking over to where Ashley stood. Laura continued to clutch a scalpel in a white-knuckled grip for all the good such a weapon would do her against one of the kaiju if one was indeed waiting beyond the door.

"You have a better plan?" Ashley asked her. "The longer we stay here, the more of a chance one the kaiju is going to find a way in, and if you haven't noticed, the power is becoming erratic too."

That part was certainly true. The lab's lights had dimmed and even flickered on and off a few times over the last few minutes.

"If the power goes out, moving through Alpha Station's corridors will get a lot harder and likely a lot more lethal too. Besides, even if we do remain here to wait on help to come, which I find more and more unlikely with each passing minute, when power does fail, we'll eventually freeze to death," Ashley pointed out.

"That would take a long, long time," Laura argued. "We have some food and more than enough water sources in the lab to last for days, maybe even weeks if we start catching it up now instead of going off halfcocked into God knows what out there."

Ashley shook her head. "You're underestimating the kaiju, Laura. They will get into this lab long before such things become an issue."

"I don't want to go out there," Dr. Pressley sobbed openly.

"Fine," Laura snapped at Ashley. "Let's say we do follow your lead. Then what do we do with the colonel? None of us can carry him alone and dragging him with us will slow us down to a crawl at best."

"I didn't say I had all the answers," Ashley spat back at her. "But you know I'm right. It's either die trying to get out or die sitting here waiting on those things to come to us. At least with my plan, there is a chance some of us will make it topside."

"We can't just leave the colonel, you know?" Laura said. "That would be murder."

"And what he did... Sending his men into the kaiju corpse without giving us the time we needed to make sure it would be safe... That's very likely murdered us all," Ashley reminded her.

"Still doesn't make it right for us to leave him," Laura replied, standing her ground.

"I would say that's relative," Ashley said.

Ashley turned to Dr. Pressley. "I know you don't want to leave the lab but trust me, if we stay, we're as good as dead. You're a bloody scientist, so start acting like one. You know that I'm right if you look at things logically."

Dr. Pressley slowly and very reluctantly nodded. "I'll go with you."

"Glad that's settled," Ashley quipped. "Now, Dr. Pressley, you're going to have to cast the deciding vote on what to do about the colonel. Do we leave him or try to carry him with us?"

"Hey!" Laura snapped. "Look at him!" She pointed at Dr. Pressley. "He's in no shape to make that kind of call and you know it."

"He's alive and he's got as much on the line as either of us," Ashley spat Laura. "That gives him a voice in this argument too."

Dr. Pressley's voice was a whimper as he spoke up, "We have to leave him, Laura. We can send help if we make it out ,but if we try to take him …"

"It's decided," Ashley said, firmly glaring at Laura. "Two against one says he stays."

"Then I'm not going," Laura said.

"And that would make you an idiot," Ashley snarled. "If you want to stay here and die, that's your call. Come on, Pressley, we're getting out of here."

Ashley pressed her ear to the door again. There was still nothing but silence coming from its other side. She glanced over at Dr. Pressley. "You ready?"

"Not really, but if we're going, let's do it and get it over with," he answered.

Ashley nodded and opened the lab's door. She started to scream as she found herself staring into the eyes of a kaiju. It had been waiting there the whole time. The beast stood completely silent and motionless, its gaze fixed onto her for a fraction of a second that passed like an eternity before it began to move. So fast that the movement appeared as little more than a blur to her, the kaiju's hand lashed outward, catching her by the backside of her head. A trio of clawed fingers snaked through her hair as they pulled her face forward towards its open, distended maw of a mouth. The bones of her cheeks crunched as razor-like teeth sunk through them.

****

Laura watched Ashley's body thrashing about in the kaiju's grip as the monster bit into her face like an apple. The fire extinguisher Ashley had been holding clanged to the lab's floor and rolled away from her.

Dr. Pressley started screaming as he backed away from the door and the monster beyond it. The kaiju dropped Ashley's twitching body, springing over it, at him. Somehow, Dr. Pressley found the presence of mind to snatch up a nearby chair and bring it around in an arc at the kaiju. The chair shattered as the kaiju blocked it with its right forearm. The chair did give the kaiju pause though. Laura ran up to it, stabbing the blade of her scalpel into the side of its neck. Such a blow would have been lethal to a human at least in the long run, but the kaiju didn't seem too badly bothered by it. It reached up taking hold of the scalpel and ripped it out of its scales. The scalpel snapped apart between the kaiju's clawed fingers as the beast broke it over the top of its middle one.

The colonel came suddenly awake in his chair. "What the...?" he rasped before the kaiju charged him. Colonel Pitt's eyes went wide as the kaiju plunged its hand into and through his ribcage. The kaiju's hand jerk its way back out clutching Colonel Pitt's still-beating heart. Seemingly unconcerned with her and Dr. Pressley, the monster paused to sink its teeth into the blood-filled organ. It wolfed down the heart, swallowing it in two bites.

Laura flung herself toward the fire extinguisher where it lay as Dr. Pressley turned to run deeper into the lab. He had only made it a few steps before the kaiju stopped him. It tackled him from behind like a football player, crashing to the floor of the lab with him in its grasp. Dr. Pressley's balled-up fists beat at the monster's shoulders as it held him down and lowered its face closer to his own as it gave a loud hiss like a ticked-off snake.

Dr. Pressley was dead before Laura could even get the fire extinguisher aimed at the monster. It tore out the man's throat in an explosion of blood that sent red splattering across the lab.

Squeezing the fire extinguisher's trigger, Laura hosed the monster, hoping to drive it away from Dr. Pressley and herself. The stream of cold had no effect on the monster whatsoever beyond making it snarl in a new burst of anger. It jumped at her. Its clawed hands slashed through the air, one raking over each of her thighs. Laura wailed as she felt her flesh and the muscles beneath it tear. The creature veered away at the last instant instead of landing on top her as she collapsed. The extinguisher bounced away from her as she thudded to the floor. She reached for it in desperation rolling onto her side after it. The kaiju grabbed her outstretched arm and snapped the bone inside of it. She flopped over onto her back again, pounding at the kaiju with her last functional limb as it crawled to rest on its knees over her. It calmly caught her by the wrist beneath her balled-up fist and smashed her good arm into the floor with such force that the bones there were reduced to mush beneath her skin. She realized that the beast had essentially hobbled her and could now take its time in doing whatever it wanted.

A long, forked tongue lolled out of its mouth. Its cold wetness caressed the skin of her cheeks and worked its way over her lips. Laura spat into the monster's face. It was all that she had left that she could do. The tongue swiped her saliva from its scales and then came at her lips again. She tried to keep them shut against the intruding tongue. Its strength overpowered hers though and her lips parts as the forked, cold mass slid between her lips. Laura made sickening choking sounds for a long, long time before she finally died.

****

Agent Markson and Sam ducked as bullets pinged and sparked off the wall behind where they had been only moments before.

"Stop shooting!" Agent Markson yelled. "We're humans, you idiot!"

The two of them had just reached the lift to the surface when someone had opened up on them from the bend in the corridor to the left. Sam saw that the shooter was the woman he had met his first night in Alpha Station. He remembered her name clearly. No man ever forgot a woman that looked like she did.

"Caroline!" Sam shouted. "It's me! Sam! The cryptozoologist guy!"

Caroline's rifle fell silent. "Sam?" she called out.

Sam stood up slowly. "Yeah, it's me."

Caroline appeared as if she was about to cry. "You're fragging lucky I ran out of ammo for my AA-12 before I got here," she told him, "or you'd be in bits and pieces right now."

Agent Markson had scrambled to his feet as well. He kept the barrel of his pistol leveled at Caroline until she lowered her rifle.

"You're Lieutenant Edwards, right?" Agent Markson asked, looking her up and down.

"I am. I can't believe someone else made it up here," she said, shaking her head in disbelief.

"She's one of our pilots, Sam," Agent Markson told him, grinning.

"I know," Sam said, smirking back at him. "We've met."

Agent Markson glanced from one of them to the other. "Well, I am afraid your reunion is going to have to wait. We need to get topside before another one of those monsters stumbles onto us."

"That lift working?" Caroline asked. "The ones below aren't."

"Don't know," Agent Markson answered. "We were about to try it when someone started shooting at us."

"Sorry about that," Caroline said, shrugging. "A girl can't be too careful in an arctic base infested with nightmare beasts straight out of Hell."

"Kaiju don't come from Hell," Sam started to explain.

"Not now, Sam," Agent Markson warned him, starting for the lift. Its doors were shut tight. "Give me a hand here."

"Uh uh," Caroline said. "Get Sam to do it. I'll cover the two of you."

Sam hurried over to help Agent Markson with the lift's doors. The two of them together managed to get them open.

"Going up?" Sam laughed, gesturing for Caroline to head into the lift.

Caroline, rifle at the ready, entered the lift carefully. It was clear of kaiju. Agent Markson and Sam followed her into it.

"It's got power," Agent Markson commented.

"Great," Caroline said, staring at him. "But does it work?"

Agent Markson stabbed at the lift's control panel with his pointer finger. The lift's doors shuddered and then finally slid closed. "Kind of," he answered, smiling at her.

"Guess that's going to have to be good enough," she said with a laugh.

"Take us up then," Sam said.

Agent Markson hit the button to take them topside. The lift lurched as it started moving. It rose slowly upwards in its shaft until it finally clanged to a stop and its doors tried to open. They stopped after only cracking a foot or so apart.

Caroline, Sam, and Agent Markson all looked at each other.

"Well, someone is going to have to get them the rest of the way open," Caroline said at last.

"Right then," Sam agreed. "I'm the most expendable. I'll do it."

Agent Markson stopped him. "Hold up there, Doc. What makes you think you've suddenly become expendable? If anything, you're more valuable now than ever. You've seen the things here up close and personal. The folks back home are going to need that mind of yours if there are more of these things out there like the ones here."

"He's right, Sam," Caroline agreed. "Step back and let us do it."

Sam watched as the two of them managed to fight the lift's doors apart. Sam recognized the corridor they opened into as the one he had first come through on his way into

Alpha Station. He knew at its other end was a door to the outside world and the sharp coldness of the arctic beyond.

Something slammed into the bottom of the lift, jarring it upwards. Sam caught himself as he lost his balance, bracing himself against the wall of the lift to stay on his feet. Agent Markson wasn't as lucky. The agent toppled onto his butt as Caroline staggered out of the lift into the corridor.

"It's a kaiju!" Agent Markson told them. "It has to be."

"Mother pus bucket," Sam shouted as a clawed hand shot upwards through the floor of the lift, its claws swiping about blindly.

"Go on, Sam," Agent Markson ordered him. "You two get out of here. I'll see to this thing."

Agent Markson's Desert Eagle roared, blowing two of the hand's clawed fingers from it in a mess of splattering black blood and tearing scales.

"I said go, Sam!" Agent Markson reached over to shove Sam into the corridor.

Sam felt Caroline's hands grab him from behind and hurl him on passed her. She didn't give him the chance to look back as she kept shoving him forward.

"He made his choice, Sam!" she raged at him. "We have to keep moving so that it wasn't in vain!"

****

The two of them stumbled out into the cold. Neither of them was fully prepared for it. It took Sam's breath and he struggled to get it back as Caroline kept him moving. She led him to a camouflaged, military helicopter. Sam didn't know enough about helicopters to know what kind it was, but it looked sleek and lethal as Caroline cleared away the tarps concealing it.

"Get inside," she shouted at him as she finished up her work.

"Shouldn't we try for one of the other buildings first?" Sam stuttered at her as shivers racked his body and he held his arms folded up about his body.

"They're on fire, Sam," she said, gawking at him.

"Wha...?" Sam took a look around and saw that she was right. The other two buildings near the shed like one they had emerged from were indeed on fire. The one he had thought was a power station as he arrived was barely more than a smoking hole in the snow. Glowing embers and smoke rose from it on the arctic winds. The other larger building was a raging inferno. That had to mean the kaiju had made it topside too and before them.

"We've got to get in the air, Sam," Caroline pleaded with him. "Get in the fragging bird already."

Sam climbed into the co-pilot seat as Caroline climbed in beside him, sliding on the helmet that had been sitting in the seat. Her fingers flew over panels of controls, apparently prepping the helicopter for flight.

"Hold on," she told him as a snarling pair of kaiju emerged from the lift building and began to sprint through the snow towards the helicopter.

The helicopter rose upwards, barely escaping the grabbing hands of the two creatures and then soared away from the base on a northward heading.

"We did it, Sam," Caroline said, grinning at him. "We really made it out."

"Thanks to you," Sam agreed with a smile of his own.

Caroline was already shouting out a distress call over the mic of her pilot's helmet.

Sam's smile curled into an expression of terror as he looked back out of the helicopter's window towards the location of Alpha Station. Something was stirring behind the snow, and whatever it was, it was big enough to be causing the ground there to buckle and rise upwards.

"Oh God, please no..." Sam muttered as the horror he had seen vanished from his line of sight and the helicopter flew on northward.

END

Read on for a free sample of

Eric S Brown is the author of numerous book series including the Bigfoot War series, the Kaiju Apocalypse series (with Jason Cordova), the Crypto-Squad series (with Jason Brannon), the Homeworld series (With Tony Faville and Jason Cordova), the Jack Bunny Bam series, and the A Pack of Wolves series. Some of his stand alone books include War of the Worlds plus Blood Guts and Zombies, World War of the Dead, Last Stand in a Dead Land, Sasquatch Lake, Kaiju Armageddon, Megalodon, Megalodon Apocalypse, Kraken, Alien Battalion, The Last Fleet, and From the Snow They Came to name only a few. His short fiction has been published hundreds of times in the small press in beyond including markets like the Onward Drake and Black Tide Rising anthologies from Baen Books, the Grantville Gazette, the SNAFU Military horror anthology series, and Walmart World magazine. He has done the novelizations for such films as Boggy Creek: The Legend is True (Studio 3 Entertainment) and The Bloody Rage of Bigfoot (Great Lake films). The first book of his Bigfoot War series was adapted into a feature film by Origin Releasing in 2014. Werewolf Massacre at Hell's Gate was the second of his books to be adapted into film in 2015. Major Japanese publisher, Takeshobo, recently bought the reprint rights to his Kaiju Apocalypse series (with Jason Cordova) and it is slated for 2018 release in Japan. Ring of Fire Press will be releasing a collected edition of his Monster Society stories (set in the New York Times Best-selling world of Eric Flint's 1632) later this year. In addition to his fiction, Eric also writes an award winning comic book news column entitled "Comics in a Flash." Eric lives in North Carolina with his wife and two children where he continues to write tales of the hungry dead, blazing guns, and the things that lurk in the woods.

Kaiju Rampage

Captain Daichi watched his crew hard at work on the deck of the *Hiroaka*. The day had just begun, but already the ship's hold was filling up with fish from her nets. Daichi had never seen the kind of loads his men were hauling now before in his life. It was almost as if something out there in the water was driving the fish his way. He whispered a prayer of thanks and smiled. This was Daichi's first run as captain. He had feared he would not live up to the expectations of his father and let the old man down. Even at the age of thirty-one, Daichi was somewhat afraid of the old man. Though his father was pushing eighty, he could still make his words cut deeper than the sharpest of swords.

The two of them had never seen eye to eye. Daichi had never wanted to be a part of his father's fishing company, much less the captain of the old man's best remaining boat. Daichi had dreamed of being a writer, going to America, and becoming a star. At first, he had some success. He had sold his first ever story to a paying magazine and almost immediately got an offer to write one for another. That sort of thing was rare in the writing world, and Daichi allowed himself to believe that he could make it. He spent the next few years doing his best. His work sold, he made money, but it was never quite enough or dependable enough to be all he did in terms of a job.

Daichi's father had been there for him, if at a price. His father had given him just enough work to keep him afloat and chasing his dream for a time. After five years had passed, his father became more and more demanding of him, pushing more and more work onto him. His father's health had begun to fail with age. The old man needed someone who could take over and continue to bring honor to the family name. Daichi was the only son. He had three sisters, but his father wanted him, not them. His father held with the old ways and wanted Daichi to surrender his failed dream to step up and do what he had been born to do.

When this fishing season had started, the old man had given Daichi a choice. Take over as captain of the *Hiroaka* or leave the family business behind for good. Daichi had known it was no idle threat. Either he stepped up or he was out. His self-published sales were down, and short stories weren't paying what they used to, not that it had ever been enough. With his rent already close to being late and a stack of bills on his desk, Daichi was left with no choice. Now, here he was on the deck of the *Hiroaka*, doing the job he had sworn as a child he would never do.

The *Hiroaka* was an old ship, only weighing in at a displacement of around one hundred and fifty tons. Her entire crew, counting Daichi himself, was composed of two dozen sailors. She ran nearly one hundred feet from bow to stern. What she lacked in size and crew, though, she more than made up for in the tech aboard her. Her sonar and comm. gear was top of the line. That fact was one of the few things Daichi liked about her.

Natsuo approached him wearing a concerned expression that gave Daichi cause for worry.

"Good morning, Natsuo," Daichi offered.

"Captain Daichi, sir," Natsuo responded with a quick nod of his head. "I would be most grateful if you would accompany me inside."

"Is my father calling again?" Daichi asked. His old man, though wheelchair bound, had followed him to sea in a sense, thanks to the very state of the art gear that Daichi liked that the *Hiroaka* had onboard. Even in the worst of storms, the ship's communications worked flawlessly.

"No, Captain Daichi," Natsuo told him. "There is something you must see."

Daichi grunted his consent and moved to follow Natsuo to the heart of the small ship where her helm controls and sonar station were. Tomo, the ship's comm. and sonar specialist, was there waiting for them. Tomo got up from his station as Daichi entered. He gave Daichi a quick bow of respect.

"What is it, Tomo?" Daichi asked. "Natsuo has been rather vague about why you needed me here."

"With good cause, Captain," Tomo said. "We did not want to cause a panic."

Daichi's eyebrows rose at the bizarre disclosure. "Panic? What are you talking about, Tomo?"

"Look for yourself, sir," Tomo told him, gesturing at the sonar screen.

Daichi studied the screen. At first, he didn't have a clue what Tomo was trying to show him, but then he saw it. The blip was so large Daichi had thought it was just part of the screen.

"What is that?" he asked.

"We don't know, Captain," Natsuo told him. "Whatever it is, though, it's coming straight for us."

"And fast, too," Tomo added. "It's moving at twenty knots."

Daichi glanced back at the sonar screen, quickly doing the math in his head. "So we have about ten minutes until whatever that is reaches us?"

Tomo and Natsuo nodded in unison.

"Could it be a ship?" Daichi asked. "Have you tried hailing it?"

"I don't think it's a ship, sir," Tomo said. "Something about the way it moves. . ."

"We have tried making contact with it, Captain," Natsuo informed him. "On every channel available to us. There has been no reply."

Daichi rubbed at his cheeks with the fingers and thumb of his right hand. "I am man enough to admit I don't have an answer to this one. Both of you are more experienced with all this. What do you suggest we do?"

"Run, Captain," Tomo said almost instantly. "We certainly can't fight something that size and that fast if it's hostile. The *Hiroaka* is a fishing boat. Yes, we have some small arms aboard in case of pirates but nothing that could give us a chance against something like that."

"I have to agree, sir," Natsuo nodded.

"The men are in the middle of pulling up the nets," Daichi protested. "All the fish in them here will be lost if we run. And what we will tell the rest of the crew? Won't running cause exactly the sort of panic you were hoping to avoid?"

Neither Natsuo nor Tomo had an answer.

"You said this thing is moving at twenty knots correct?" Daichi asked, still weighing his course of action.

"Yes, Captain," Tomo replied.

"The *Hiroaka*'s max speed with her engines at full is only eighteen knots," Daichi reminded them. "If we run and whatever that thing is decides to come after us, we won't be able to outrun it."

Natsuo and Tomo stared at him, waiting for his orders.

"The call is yours, sir," Natsuo said. "Whatever you decide to do, though, Captain, I suggest we do it quickly."

"Fine," Daichi grunted. "Tell the crew what's going on and pass out what weapons we do have aboard. There's no point in keeping them in the dark at this point. They'll know something is badly wrong as soon as we give the order to abandon the nets."

Daichi paused, taking a breath before continuing. It hurt him to give up the fish, but he could see no other option. "Tell them to drop the nets. Tomo, get down to the engines and make sure we get all the speed out of them that we can. Natsuo, set a course away from whatever that thing, maximum speed."

Tomo and Natsuo hurried to carry out his orders while Daichi moved to watch the chaos that began on the ship's deck as soon as Natsuo started barking orders through the loudspeakers.

The crew outside looked absolutely terrified as they cut loose the nets they had been reeling up. He could see in their faces, even from where he was looking out the window of the small control room of the ship. The fear in those expressions only grew as Natsuo ordered the men to pass out the weapons from the ship's weapon lockers.

Daichi's attention became focused on the horizon beyond the *Hiroaka*'s forward deck. He picked up a nearby pair of binoculars and raised them to his eyes. Out there in the distance, he could see the something massive cutting through the waves towards the ship. Daichi felt sick as the full scale of its size sunk in. The thing was many, many times the size of the *Hiroaka*.

Natsuo was spinning the wheel around madly, turning the *Hiroaka* away from the approaching contact. Daichi could already see that even with the engines straining at full power, it wasn't going to be enough.

Some of the sailors on the deck who had already been given small arms opened fire at the massive creature streaking towards the ship. Shotguns thundered and pistols cracked rapid succession. Daichi had to bite his lip to keep from laughing at how futile their shots seemed given the size of the thing coming at them.

In the last instant before the creature plowed into the *Hiroaka*, it rose partially up out of the waves. Its head was horned. A great horn protruded from each side of its skull, and a third larger one rose from the middle of its forehead. Its body was covered in thick scales that reminded Daichi of the scales of python, all yellow and black. It gave a roar that left everyone aboard the *Hiroaka* screaming in pain and clutching their ears before the creature dropped its head back into the water. The window in front of Daichi blew out. Shards of glass exploded, burying them in his flesh. Blood spurted in splashes of bright red from one piece ripped open the side of his neck. Daichi stumbled backwards to collapse onto the floor.

The monster struck the *Hiroaka* at a speed well over twenty knots. The hull of the fishing vessel folded inward with the squeals of rending metal. The impact was so great that the *Hiroaka* was lifted from the surface of the ocean and sent toppling over onto its side before it completely broke apart as the monster plowed through it, tearing it to pieces.

Kaiju Rampage is available from Amazon here!

CHECK OUT OTHER GREAT KAIJU NOVELS

ATOMIC REX: WRATH OF THE POLAR YETI
by Matthew Dennion

It has been fifteen years since Captain Chris Myers used his giant mech to draw the kaiju of North America into each other's territory to have them destroy each other. Once all of the kaiju had battled to the death only Atomic Rex was left standing. In Antarctica, the kaiju known as Armorsaur has entered the frozen valley of the yetis and attacked them. Devouring all but one alpha male yeti who was exposed to the kaiju's blood and left dying in the snow. The yeti awoke to find himself transformed into a kaiju with an obsession to destroy Armorsaur. Chris and Kate are forced to protect the people of their settlement by drawing Atomic Rex into South America where he will battle the kaiju there to usurp their territory and claim their hunting grounds as his own. As Atomic Rex enters South America from the north the enraged Polar Yeti enters the continent from the south. The two most powerful kaiju in the world will battle their way through a multitude of giant monsters as they are set on a collision course with each other!

KAIJU CORPS
by Matthew Dennion

They are four soldiers who were genetically created to be mankind's last line of defense against potential world ending threats. They are soldiers who can transform themselves into gigantic monsters. They are the Kaiju Corps and they are facing a threat that is beyond the scope of even their fantastic abilities.

CHECK OUT OTHER GREAT KAIJU NOVELS

POLAR YETI AND THE BEASTS OF PREHISTORY
by Matthew Dennion

A team from Princeton University searching for a lost tribe in Antartica discover a hidden valley filled with wooly mammoths, saber toothed tigers and other Ice Age beasts. Seizing the opportunity of a lifetime, the team set up camp to study the amazing creatures. But there is something else that lives in the Valley. Something terrifying. Something beyond imagination. POLAR YETI!

TITAN WARS
by M.C. Norris

Millions of microscopic alien life forms escape a sample canister of water from the frigid depths of outer space. Invisible to the naked eye, a menacing menagerie of more than seventy deadly species react to Earth's warm and fertile seas by launching into metabolic overdrive. Waves of gargantuan abominations begin to rise from the sea, transforming our world into a zoo without cages, where humans plunge to the bottom of the food chain.

In dire need of a zookeeper, the Allied Navy turns to "Psyjack," a bickering geek squad with an outrageous plan to hack into the minds of the megafauna with some reengineered neurosurgical technology. The young gamers hope to level the uneven playing field by fighting monsters with monsters, but they couldn't have anticipated how deadly their technology could be, if it ever fell into the wrong hands ...

SEVERED**PRESS**

CHECK OUT OTHER GREAT KAIJU NOVELS

KAIJU WINTER
by Jake Bible

The Yellowstone super volcano has begun to erupt, sending North America into chaos and the rest of the world into panic. People are dangerous and desperate to escape the oncoming mega-eruption, knowing it will plunge the continent, and the world, into a perpetual ashen winter. But no matter how ready humanity is, nothing can prepare them for what comes out of the ash: Kaiju!

RAIJU
by K.H. Koehler

His home destroyed by a rampaging kaiju, Kevin Takahashi and his father relocate to New York City where Kevin hopes the nightmare is over. Soon after his arrival in the Big Apple, a new kaiju emerges. Qilin is so powerful that even the U.S. Military may be unable to contain or destroy the monster. But Kevin is more than a ragged refugee from the now defunct city of San Francisco. He's also a Keeper who can summon ancient, demonic god-beasts to do battle for him, and his creature to call is Raiju, the oldest of the ancient Kami. Kevin has only a short time to save the city of New York. Because Raiju and Qilin are about to clash, and after the dust settles, there may be no home left for any of them!

www.ingramcontent.com/pod-product-compliance
Lightning Source LLC
Chambersburg PA
CBHW052000170626

46808CB00007B/2705